The End of the World

and other stories

by

BRYAN MacMAHON

POOLBEG PRESS : DUBLIN

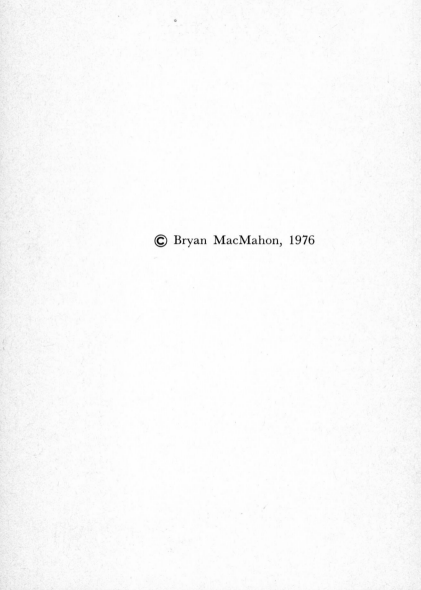

This collection first published 1976 by Poolbeg Press Ltd.,
Knocksedan House, Swords, Co. Dublin, Ireland.

Printed by The Leinster Leader Ltd., Naas, Co. Kildare

Some of the stories in this collection were chosen from *The Lion Tamer and other stories* and from *The Red Petticoat and other stories*. Others have previously appeared only in periodicals or been broadcast, and acknowledgements are due to *The Kilkenny Magazine, The Irish Press* 'New Irish Writing', the B.B.C., and Radio Telefis Eireann.

Contents

The generous assistance of An Chomhairle Ealaion: The Arts Council and of the Arts Council of Northern Ireland in the publication of this book is gratefully acknowledged.

The End of the World

We used to play games among ourselves in order to disturb the placidity of the place. Most of our games were games of pretence. That is to say, we started with tiny imaginative embers and kept blowing and blowing until we had a mythical conflagration. On rare occasions we had real flames, the annual race-meeting, the death of a prominent man, unexpected courtships, the downfall of a beautiful woman, first births and so on. But mostly the fires at which we warmed ourselves were imaginary fires, failing whose warmth and chcer some of us descended to the minor sadism of thumbing blackheads out of one another's checkbones. That, or the brutality of direct address. For it is an article of faith with us that oblique commentary is a blessed thing, not unlike the shaft of sunshine striking through the church window across which the man in the folk-story hung his jacket.

So, naturally, I was delighted when I spied the item tucked away at the bottom of a page in the newspaper. I slicked it out with a razor-blade and poked it away in my fob-pocket. When I reached the harness-maker's I took out the cutting and passed it around among the men. I gave it to the harness-maker first, as was his right as host.

The item in the newspaper said that a Rumanian (or a Hungarian or a Yugo-Slav, I forget which) had prophesied that the end of the world would come the following morning precisely at two o'clock.

Hereabouts the radio is commonplace. And from our cousins in the States we get more than our share of American magazines. We also have a pair of picture-houses. All these amenities serve us highly: if we aren't able to differentiate the seventy-seven different types of jealousy by this time, it isn't day yet. But in spite of the radio and the magazines and the cinema, the lacunae

7

in us are both surprising and formidable—lacunae which astonish even ourselves in our solitary if infrequent contemplations.

As regards the end of the world I quickly discovered that I had green faggots for my kindling. Still, I counselled myself to patience and blew assiduously at the seed of my fire.

The saddler spoke first. He said it was all his bloody eye. I felt that the wrong keynote had been sounded. The man should have rung the middle C of pleasant pretence. But we had to humour the saddler, as he held us in the hollow of his hand, inasmuch as we were dependent on him to give us sanctuary against the weather and our loneliness. He spoke with high bravado as if a show of initial sternness would, once and for all, put a stop to this tomfoolery of an end to the grand world. When I saw that pretence had been jettisoned I grew peeved. In my heart I kept protesting that it wasn't fair, that the harness-maker should have been traditional, and should have thrust slyly and obliquely at the story. I had wished us to remain knaves manufacturing knavery. Sourly I withdrew from the men, put my shoulder against the jamb of the door and tried finitely if perversely to appreciate what the world's end would mean to our town.

On the opposite side of the roadway, at the entrance to the market, a fishwoman was standing beside an open box of fish which was set upon two empty boxes. As I watched her she viced a mackerel by the gills and ran it through the O of the thumb and forefinger. Well, for one thing, the end of the world would put a stop to that sleazy antic. In the midst of my resultant good humour my mind took the bit in its teeth and ran away. Suddenly I found myself gigantic and wholly capable of ending the world myself. This I proceeded to do. I clawed down the scarlet-and-white ice-cream bannerols, banged the Mediterranean-blue whiskey signs, tangled up the old electric wires, beat immense caverns in the roadway,

kicked over the steeples, disembowelled children playing
hop-scotch, smashed pigeons into sunny slates, shredded
petunia posters, jangled plate-glass windows — finally
I rammed my fist back Mick Meenihan's throat and, once
and for all, set a period to his singing "Moon-Wine
Shimmering in Your Hair." As a postscript I crashed
down the high chittering blue hat-band in the cinema-
operator's cabin.

Sated with destruction I turned back into the shop.
Then Frankie Horan spoke up out of his wryness; whatever it was he said brought me in among the others on
the crest of a warm conversational wave. I twinkled with
miniature happiness. I cast about for a simile and found
it ready to my hand. Our humour, I thought, was like a
little shrine-lamp with a weighted base that would topple
and sway in an alarming fashion and then unaccountably
right itself. I grew ashamed of my former peevishness.
The twinkling spread among us. We booted the world
around as if it were a football. I felt wondrously proud
of myself for having brought up the matter — for having
made this pleasant warmth in our ways.

Frankie Horan said: "You must admit that the Man
Above put up with the thieves and ruffians for a long
time."

Jack Donovan said: "I leave to anyone if that's fair
talk in the presence of an honest tradesman. Twenty-five
years I'm coming in that door and I never yet saw the
saddler here put weak leather in a collar. Aye, or puttin'
fibre in the linin' of a straddle an' tellin' the unfortunate
farmers 'twas curled horse-hair."

Jim Sheehan said: "In the Hereafter if I find all of ye
in one place, I'm praying here and now that I find myself
in the other."

Mickie Duv Larkin said: "It's comin' just in the nick
o' time. I've a fishery prosecution hangin' over my head
for Saturday's court."

The saddler laughed heartily. We began to enjoy ourselves prodigiously.

All through the evening the hocus-pocus spread. Man, 'twas great! Those who weren't perturbed pretended to be perturbed. Some of the variants of the story I heard amazed even myself with the fine skin of truth they had on them. I had to show the cutting to several people who stopped me on the street. The cutting was out of an English paper I get specially for the horses. It gave the Rumanian's name down in black and white — also the things he had foretold already. Myself, now, I thought the man an honest sort of a fellow but a sort of a fool all the same. Whatever way things turned out he couldn't be much the gainer. If the end of the world didn't arrive his name would be a byword in the mouths of the people; while if it did come, there would be none of us left to hang laurels on the prophet. But I'll give it up to him and say that he thought he was acting according to his lights. And besides, it's not right for any man to set himself up as a judge of another.

About eleven o'clock that night I was sauntering home for myself, intending to be in bed for once in my life at a respectable hour. Besides, I had promised Danny Sweeney to go flood-fishing with him early the following morning. Passing Louis Fitzmaurice's hall-door I saw that it was open — I sort of sensed Louis smoking inside in the dark. The devil pinched me — I flung him good night and passed on. I made a bet with myself that he'd call me. I gave him two intervals to do so. In the first interval he was to recognize the sound of my step, gait and voice. The second interval was for the plupping apart of his his lips from around the pipe-stem preparatory to the calling of my name. I won my bet — suddenly I heard an unrehearsed "Vincent!" I slowed down and forced him to call me a second time. As I came round the door-post I adroitly switched my greeting into a yawn and did my best to muster up a counterfeit irritation. He drew slowly on his pipe. Now and again the pipelight on his face glowed and died. He smoked on, solemn as a mandarin.

"You're in a terrible hurry home, to-night," he said.

"Maybe I've cause," I said darkly.

"Seldom with you have cause," he said. "Move in for a few minutes. I won't take the head o' you."

By the light of the next pipe-brightness I examined his face. You would have known him anywhere for the publican he was. The standard mixture of solemnity and rascality. The pushed-out lugs made the face an isosceles triangle, his narrowing skull yielded a vertex in a lock of dark hair pomaded to the forehead. His finely waxed moustache fitted the geometrical verity of his face; the long slender moustache-ends bisected the base-angles at his lugs. His eyes were wonderful eyes. They were capable of the subtlest flattery by offering you their whites in exchange for your wonders.

"What's this I hear about the end of world?" he asked.

Now the pipe-brightnesses fell thick and fast upon me. My breast gladdened at the solution of a problem that had been pecking at me for many years. Now, for the first time, it was clear to me why Louis Fitz. smoked a pipe with a dropped bowl. I had always thought that it was because the weight of such a pipe was taken partly on the chin, but with a sudden access of clarity of vision I now realized that Louis Fitz.—and all the other millions of Louis Fitzes throughout the world — were men inquisitive in the extreme, and hated having the range of their vision impaired by a pipe-bowl and a fist clenched around it. I gained a new respect for Louis Fitzmaurice.

I handed him the cutting; he cracked a match to read it. He didn't ask me to turn on the electric light although at that moment I happened to be itching a dying pimple on my cheek with the button of the switch. No publican in his normal vigour and senses lights his hall-light at eleven o'clock at night, unless, God save the hearers, it's a case of a sudden death or a homecoming after an operation. Louis and myself had a bout of wrestling trying to pronounce the Rumanian's name. With the pipe-stem venting the air between his cheeks he went off into hegs of laughter at the idea of anyone having a name like that. He gave me back my cutting; I fingered it back into my fob-pocket. He took out his watch and concertinaed his chin into his chest as he tried to read the time by the light of his pipe. He made ribbons of the fine triangle of his face before he finally saw what o'clock it was.

"A quarter after eleven," he said. Then, with a sham gaiety: "That makes it two and three-quarter hours till the end of the world." I didn't laugh.

"Sit in; sit in," he said arrogantly, " 'tis seldom I have a chat with you."

There were two mahogany chairs against the wall on each side of the small hall-table. On the table was a check oil-cloth, in the middle of which was a maidenhair fern in a *jardinière*. I sat on the chair farther from the door. Louis pulled his chair across from me in order to let me see my due portion of an up-ended rectangle of moon-bright street.

The people came out from the pictures, the gods thumping lustily along the pavement, whistling cheerily as they went, the tip-ups in long swaths mincing in-hibitedly in mid-road. When the last of the people had flowed past us and things in the town were terribly silent, Louis turned the key in the shop-door and brought out two bottles of stout, a glass and an opener. He placed them on the table in front of me and partly behind the *jardinière*. " 'Tis mortal close to-night," he said.

Etiquette demanded that I say, "Tck-tck." I said it and added for good measure. "This is too much altogether."

We talked and talked. Now and again the apparition of a benevolent rosy face appeared from nowhere to

encourage me. The old rascal pretended not to have
heard stories I knew I had already told him. He made
me tell them all over again. There was nothing left for
me but to better the previous tellings. While we talked
I nursed my two bottles of stout. I knew they'd have to
last me till the end of the world. Times there were that
the stream of my narrative was filtered through
stout-froth and the maidenhair fern. By this time the
street was like a dead-house. The last noise was that of
a pony and trap jigging into the country. We saw the
flutter of a nurse's veil in it.

Louis and I kept talking on everything and anything.
We talked of heartburn, Jane Withers and the inbreeding
of rabbits; of the County Council rates and dead Canons
and the scarfing of welding-iron; of pewter and rock-salt
and the bars in Montreal; of house-leek and ptomaine
poisoning and old meadowing. But through all the trading of knowledge and the tongue-tossing of news, my
brave Mr. Louis Fitzmaurice kept nibbling and nibbling
at the end of the world.

At one o'clock I topped the second bottle: I squeezed
that out till a quarter to two. About a quarter after one
we heard a noising behind the stairs door. Louis got up
quickly, stuck his head in the doorway and commenced
whispering up the stairs. I dare say he was telling the
wife what was keeping him in the hall. When he came
back I made the decisive movements a person makes
before breaking company, but Louis broached a fresh
topic of conversation with over-zeal.

Two o'clock banged out from the steeple, and, indeed,
the world didn't come to an end. Louis and I were side
by side in the doorway when the hour rang. After the
second stroke there came a great calm. Louis looked up
at the stars. No crack appeared in the roof of the sky. I
heard no trumpet and, curiously enough, I found myself
undefinably disappointed. High up in a top room a child
began to wail — we heard the mother's voice comforting

it. The child's complaint became submerged in a reluctant wetness.

On the off-chance that the town clock was fast, Louis and myself gave the coming of doom an extra five minutes. But even after the extra five minutes everything stayed up. I left him and he closed the door softly behind me. When I found myself utterly alone in the moonlit street, I felt exhilarated beyond description, though deep in the exhilaration was the far gnaw of the disappointment that now I should never know whether the stars were merely stars or scales on the back of the Big Salmon. As I walked home I saw the walls silvered with snail tracks. At the corner of our street there was a steel electric pole. With the dint of the glee that was on me I struck it smartly with my open palm. The whole pole rang with the truth of a good bell.

When I reached home I closed the door softly behind me and tiptoed into the kitchen. Before I switched on the light I covered the switch with my two hands so as to smother the click of it. When the light went up I saw the clock-beetles that the turf had brought into us, racing clean-mad all over the floor. I hopped quickly here and there among them and, selecting the bigger clocks, I cracked them under my boots. When the last beetle had reached sanctuary I was left with five or six flattened beetles. They looked like squashed chocolate sweets on the floor.

Then I heard the creak of old ankles over my head. Even before I raised my face I knew that my mother was leaning over the banisters of the landing. We looked at one another for a while, each waiting for other to begin. "Tell me, Vincent," she said at last, "what kept you out till this hour of the morning?" Defensively I reached for my fob-pocket and took out the newspaper cutting. I held it upwards in her direction. I said: "Look, mother, a Rumanian foretold the end of the world for to-night at two o'clock, and I was below in Louis Fitzmaurice's till this very minute keeping him company." She said: "And will you tell me what in the name of goodness were ye doing there till this time?" I said: "What were we doing, mother, but waiting for the end of the world."

Against this talk the poor woman was weaponless. Then, as we eyed one another, out from their cubby-holes sneaked two mighty rogueries: the roguery that was hers to bequeath and the roguery that I had inherited. I saw my soul in an old mirror. Never afterwards in my life did I come closer to my mother than at that moment. The laughter common to our blood lay between us like a red carpet with a rich pile. The set severity of her face was marred by the tears of her feeling for me. And as she turned from me and in her bare feet padded back along the landing, I sat down, clasped my hands between my knees, and, in spite of myself, I found myself rocked and rocked with the joy and the grandeur of it all.

The Crab Tree

On a night of strong wind the spreading crabtree keeled over and collapsed with a sound half-creak, half-crash. After their breakfast of sullen silence the widower and his son prepared to clear away the tree, for it lay directly across the by-road that led to the little farmhouse.

The father — he had a faded crape on the left sleeve of his jacket, left the house first, taking with him the crosscut which glittered in the November sunlight. The son, who bore little physical resemblance to his father, followed, carrying the axe.

Reaching the spot where the tree lay, the father, without speaking, indicated that the son should first lop off the branches. The son began striking at the branches with axe blows that seemed to have venom behind them. The father, a widower, appeared by his jaunty movements to indicate a temperament much younger than that of his son, who though in his mid-twenties, seemed already cast in the role of bachelor. The father's every action also implied an amused tolerance of all the son did: there was even a sense of provocation in the way he sauntered about and appeared to comment adversely without speaking.

The morning passed. On the main road below, neighbours returning from the creamery eyed the pair curiously. They did not call out a greeting. The father did little work: he was moving about, tipping idly with the saw, now and again using it single-handed on a thin branch as if it were an awkward toy. At last when the tree was clear of encumbrances the father balanced the saw on the bole. He did so in such a manner as constituted a challenge.

The son gripped the idle handle of the saw and began to draw savagely upon it. The father worked less strenuously: all the while an amused smile played about his lips. At times he whistled tunelessly.

Cross-sections of the tree-trunk began to fall; the timber started faintly to redden the instant it was cut open.

Along the main road below, came a middle-aged woman driving a tub trap drawn by a black pony. At the mouth of the little road that led to the house she drew the pony to a halt and began to watch the two men. After a time she left the vehicle, tied the reins to a five-barred gate and walked uproad to where the father and son worked.

"God bless the work," she said when she was close to them.

Both growled a reply.

"A dreadful night of wind!" she said; then, "Lord have mercy on him, I never missed my poor husband till last night."

"You never miss the water till the well runs dry," the father said brightly.

"We can't live with men," the widow sighed. "Nor without them but as little!"

From under his bushy eyebrows the son glared up at the woman.

"So the old crabtree fell at last," the widow went on. "Will I tell ye a secret about it?"

"Do!" said the older man with a smile. The son drew on the cross-cut.

"I spent many a gay night under its branches with your brother Jim that's now in New Jersey."

"You did?" said the father.

"Seventeen I was at the time. Books wouldn't give down of how wild I was. But that's over and done with now."

"Often an old chimney caught fire!" the father warned.

"True for you, Patrick!" the widow laughed. "They say that the older the fiddle the sweeter the tune."

The young man paused to scowl up at the pair. The scowl told the widow to be off: it also told the father to respect himself. The woman folded her arms and settled herself as for a long gossip.

"Will I tell ye something else?" she enquired. " 'Tis often I came up here in the autumn and brought home a pillowslip of fruit to make crab apple jelly."

"There hasn't been much fruit on that tree these years past," the father said.

"And why not?"

"Because it was a female crabtree!"

"Was it now?"

"Aye! And there wasn't a male crabtree within miles of it. Except, of course, the one on the hill above your own place."

"You'll be telling me next that this crabtree died of lonesomeness."

"In one way it did!"

"What way was that?"

"It had no other tree to . . . to pollinate it."

"To pollinate it! That's a word you must explain to me."

"Inside the flowers of this crabtree there are what are called in botany — ovules. They need pollen from the stamens of a male tree before they can produce fruit."

"Are you saying that that old crabtree of mine waddled down the hill and along the road until it came up here to what-do-you-call-it, pollinate the flowers of your female crabtree?"

"Not at all, woman! The bees did that."

"The bees?"

"Aye. First of all the bees bored into the flowers on your male crabtree and then they flew across the countryside. Still dusty with your pollen, they nosed deep into the flowers of our crabtree. Everything was right then for fruit to be formed! But the day some scoundrel knocked your crabtree, Hanna, we did no good over here."

"Grip the bloody cross-cut!" the son said with a shout at his father and a scowl at the widow. With a wink at the widow, the father did so. The son began to jerk the blade of the saw towards him while the father did little more than draw the saw back towards himself.

The widow watched the work with what appeared to be a profound sense of puzzled interest.

"Well, well, well," she said at last. "And to think that all that tree-coortin' was going on under my very nose! And that I didn't know one word about it!"

Sweat gleaming on his forehead, the son again glared at his meek father and at the still meeker widow.

Just then there was a call from the road below. Looking down, all three saw a young woman dismounting from a bicycle. "Aunt Hanna," the young woman sang out. "I'm going to the shop: I'll be home soon."

"Come up here, Ellen," the widow said.

After a puzzled pause, the girl came wheeling her bicycle. For a while, the two women watched the men working. Sections of the tree continued to fall. The father greeted the young woman with a smile which he transferred to his son who was working with bent head: the smile altered subtly as it travelled through the air: it spoke of innocence that was really ignorance. The smile could be interpreted as an appeal to the wisdom of women.

"They were telling me an interesting story," the widow began solemnly, "about their female crabtree withering away for want of pollen from the male crabtree that grew in our upper field. What do you say to that, Ellen?"

The young woman said nothing. Her alive eyes were watching the movements of the young man. "And to think," the widow went on, "that crabtrees have notions much the same as ourselves."

The son stopped working. He looked up at the widow. "Have you nothing better to do this hour of the day besides upsetting men who are working?" he asked sharply.

"Your're not upsetting me, Hanna," the father said equably. "What are we doing but exchanging a few sociable words on the intricate ways of nature! Imagine our crabtree pining away for lack of company of the opposite sex — remarkable is the only word to describe it."

"To hell with it!" the son shouted, raising his handle of the saw and slamming the tool down against the trunk of the crabtree. Turning on his heel he crashed through the branches and clumped back towards the cottage. At the door he turned and shouted, "And my mother hardly cold in her grave!"

The three looked at each other. For a while no one spoke. "A hot-tempered fellah to be sure," the widow said with a small note of victory in her voice. "But then again, what use is a young man without a bit of game in him."

"He'll get over it!" the father said.

The young woman appeared thoughtful.

"I wouldn't like to come between father and son," the widow said, "so we'll be off — the pair of us. Good day to you, Patrick."

"Good day to ye," said Patrick.

"Just the same," the widow said with second-thoughts in her voice, "it wouldn't be proper to part bad friends with you or your fine boy." With a shrewd glance at the father she ordered, "Go on up you, Ellen, and apologise on behalf of the two of us."

"It might only make him worse!" the niece said.

"Not at all!" the father said. "The disease he has, it has to get worse before it gets better. Go on up, girl, and soften him out. Cry if you have to. We'll give the pair of ye plenty time."

The girl paused for a moment, then placed her bike against the hedge, and walked towards the doorway. After a pause she entered the house. The widow and the widower were left alone.

"You're a contrivin' slut," the widower said.

"Amn't I now!"

"You're watching that chance for a long time."

"You played your cards well yourself."

"My brother, Jim, in New Jersey! He never laid a finger on you."

"Didn't he, now?"

" 'Twas myself had your rump against the bole of that crabtree. And well you know it."

"How could I have mixed ye up?"

"What's on your mind?" the father demanded.

The widow paused for a long while. Then: "You to come west. She to come here," she said quietly.

The man rolled his tongue about in his mouth. "Decency requires time," he said.

"Decency you'll get — and a bit to spare."

"Hm!" Then: "It's a bargain. Providin' the pair inside have made headway."

"They'll make headway."

"You have her schooled?"

"Aye!" After a pause: "How long is it now since Old Master Torpey taught us that botany lesson? I was sitting beside you that day, Patrick. Remember?"

The widower laughed aloud. "I forget," he said at last. Then: "Come on till we see how things are progressing."

Approaching the door the widow said loudly: "They have Night Classes in the Technical School to teach you all about these subjects."

"Have they now?" Patrick answered.

Entering the kitchen the widow caught her niece's eye: her own eye glittered in answering satisfaction.

"Would ye be offended," the widow asked meekly of the two men, "if I asked Ellen here to wet a mouthful of tea for the four of us. She's a marvellous housekeeper!"

"Fire away, girl!" the father said. Then in abdication: "Of course, it's up to Joseph."

"What do you say, Joseph? You're the boss now," the

widow was addressing the son.

"The tea caddy is over there."

Later, Ellen poured out the tea. The four sat at the table. Before they began to drink, the widow raised her cup. Her eyes alight with triumph and mischief she said:

"To the crabtree!"

"To the crabtree!" the other three answered. Through the steam of his tea, the father looked at his son. Seeing that the young man's eyes were fast on the girl the father looked at the widow. The older pair sighed together in deep satisfaction.

Ballintierna in the Morning

One clear cold morning in November two young men boarded a south-bound train in Kingsbridge Station, Dublin. Both were bareheaded and wore shabby tweed overcoats. That they were fitters was a fact indicated by a black timber attaché case which one of the men was carrying; there were also tell-tale smudges of grease on their cuffs and on the edges of their overcoat pockets. Their names were Bernie Byrne and Arthur Lowe: they were being sent by their firm to repair the boiler of a country Creamery in County Kildare.

Byrne was an albino; his complexion was over-fresh and his eyes were the eyes of a tamed white rodent. His hair was cut short to avoid attracting undue attention, but the irrepressible pink of his body had bubbled up through his scalp. His expression had a disconcerting trick of trading idiocy for sagacity at the most unexpected moments. Arthur Lowe's face gave promise of being cadaverous before he was twenty-five. He had a facial tic. He was so sallow that one could not imagine his intestines to be other than grey rubber tubes. His humour, of which he was extremely niggardly, was slow, droll and deliberate. His dyspepsia, already chronic, had made him a person subject to sudden bouts of unreasoning irritation.

During the journey down—a bare hour's run—they remained standing in the corridor with their elbows resting on the horizontal guard-bar of a window. Since they were young, they resented the fact that they were wearing their working clothes while travelling—this was the reason that they did not enter a compartment. The corridor was ammoniac and stale and had little to offer them except the beginnings of train-queasiness. Despite this they found the ride slightly exhilarating, and it was with an unmistakable, if indeed somewhat subdued, sense of adventure that they looked out into the widening day. People passing to the lavatory crushed by them with barely articulated apologies. The young men gave room with excessive readiness as if to compensate with manners what they lacked in clothes. Looking downwards at an angle of forty-five degrees Byrne saw in the compartment behind him a sickish girl of four or five who was mouthing biscuits. The compartment was crowded; at a station he heard a stout woman praise the virtues of Aylesbury ducks. Some time afterwards he heard a voice from the other side of the compartment begin: "There's nothing on earth the matter with my husband, but . . ."

The men alighted at a small station in County Kildare. An impish boy of twelve with a red head and a freckled face met them. That he was a playboy was instantly obvious. His face cracked up with contagious glee as he asked:

"Are ye the men to mend the Creamery?"

"We are!"

The albino was laughing. The boy's face set for a moment as he examined Byrne's face and eyes. The albino resented the examination.

"The manager says I'm to show ye the way. If ye like, I'll get the case sent up in a Creamery car and ye can take the short-cut across the bog?"

"Across the bog?"

"Aye!"

"That'll suit me fine," said Byrne.

The boy roared at the porter who, on closer inspection, proved also to have a red head and was obviously a brother of the guide: "Hey, Mick, send that up in the next car!"

When they came out of the station they saw the trees. From an old oak depended the tattered remnants of summer finery now eked out in ragged brown bunting;

a mendicant beech held out in emaciated hands the last of its unspent coppers; the furze was flecked with in-between-season gold. Beneath the trees they saw the bogland. As they approached it they lost interest in the trees and were taken with the as yet finite landscape. Following the boy they crossed the fence between the trees and were then on the floor of the bog.

Before them a turf bank reared itself in a great black rectangular box with planed-away corners. Drawing near they saw that, close to the surface, this rampart had crazied into fissures that had oozed irregularly shaped knobs of semi-dried peat. Clean rushes in tight clumps sprang from the chocolate-coloured ground. Bog-holes were filled with ink or quicksilver according to the light's quirk. A not repulsive odour of old sulphur came up out of the mould underfoot.

Their guide was agility itself. He sprang to a step in the black bog-wall, gained purchase and leaped up. The two young men followed. Then they saw the country-side in its entirety. It had all the variety of a display of tweeds in a shop window. Under their feet it was prune and orange and vermilion, with sometimes a lichen blazing up in a brilliant green. The leathery heather swished hungrily around their boots. The large white bones of fallen and stripped trees were flung here and there in the canyons of the cutaway. The sun had bleached them and the wind had antlered them. Two or three newly erected labourers' cottages were placed around the periphery of the bog: what with their red roofs, green doors, white walls and tarred plinths they had a wholly fictitious prettiness. A disconsolate black cow moved dully beside each of these dwellings. The sky was a wash of grey clouds. On the near horizon they saw the scarlet and white hulk of the Creamery. Beyond it were the crisp orthodox hills of the Irish skyline.

The men strode along, singularly braced by the morning air. To breathe it was in itself an adventure. Since

the ground underfoot was reasonably dry they had the
sensation of walking on eiderdowns. On their left they
saw a hollow square carpeted with *fionnán* as white as
wood fibre. It was growing in great tufts which were
heavily matted in one another. The hollow seemed as
snug as the bottom of a delf-crate. Their guide dropped
into this hollow, at the same time signalling to the men
not to make unnecessary noise. Byrne and Lowe followed
warily. The youngster had his hands extended with the
palms turned backwards. He was tiptoeing forward, his
pert head turning this way and that. Suddenly he stood
stockstill and the wings of his nostrils widened. His
eyes were fixed on a tuft of grass before him. Seeing
him standing thus the two men halted. Then the boy
threw himself forward on the ground. Lying prone he
scrambled into a ball, bringing his knees up to him and
clawing at his belly. The men heard a squeal coming
from beneath the boy. For all the world it sounded like
the complaint of an injured infant.

"I have him! I have him! I so-hoed the hare!" The
youngster's voice was blotched with an excitement which
immediately communitcated itself to the men who began
to laugh and query eagerly. Lowe's tic began to beat
furiously. Meanwhile the little actor was making the
most of his moment on the stage. He rolled over to his
knees, thence to his feet, all the while clutching something in the pit of his stomach. Then the men saw the
elongated whitish body trimmed with red-brown fur.
They saw the cut and carve of the great hind legs, the
squashed ears and the huge protuberant eyes. Carefully
the boy gathered the animal together, all the while keeping the hind legs under firm control.

All three grew strangely intimate after sharing this
experience together. With a nod of his head the boy
indicated the hare's form in the grass. The albino
immediately crouched and bared the snug little arch.
They all saw where the bones of the hare's buttocks had

bared the dark clay. Byrne and Lowe in turn placed
the backs of their hands on the floor of the form and
remarked that it was still warm. As they stood up, each
man shrank and shrank in imagination until he was a
hare in the form peering out at the world through the
tangled stems of the grasses.

Then Bernie Byrne asked: "Hey! what are you going
to do with him?"

This was a question the boy had not asked himself
previously. He took refuge in a laughing vagueness. But
the actor in him suddenly provided the answer.

"I don't know . . . unless I kill him!"

"Will you give him to me?" asked the albino.

"Alive?"

"Yes, alive!"

"Sure I'll give him to you. I'll put him in a bag above
at the Creamery and you can take him with you."

Arthur Lowe had recovered his moroseness. "What
do you want him for?"

"I don't know . . . . I'll do something with him."
Byrne smiled and grew remote. This withdrawal irked
Lowe who said, "Come on or we'll never get this job
done."

It was night when they returned to the city. A frosty
river-wind caused them to shudder as they emerged
from the station. Arthur Lowe was carrying the timber
case: Byrne had the hare in a bag. They took a bus to
O'Connell Bridge.

Looking up the great thoroughfare, Byrne suddenly
discovered that he had been granted the power to view
his city with novel eyes. For one thing the balusters of
the bridge were now wondrously white. The diffused
light in the street was almost as impalpable as floating
powder: it hung in a layer perhaps twenty feet in height
and then it fined upwards into the windless city rigging.
Over this was the unremembered night sky. Dan

O'Connell himself and his satellites in bronze had all fused to form a drowsy octopus; Nelson was a cold hero on an eminence waiting to be quickened by a brilliant anecdote. The trams were lively enough, but they had gone to great pains to conceal their pattering feet. To the left and right Neon displayed its inability to form a right angle. Now and again a ragamuffin wind, shot with gaseous green slime, clambered up the ladders in the river walls and shrugged its facile way in and out of the arcades and the ice-cream parlours. The curves of the lamp-standards interpreted benevolence in terms of cement.

The people, too, had altered. In a remote nook in the street cerulean lanterns were busy transforming the passers-by into death's heads. The theatre queues were composed of sexless, friendless, kinless persons who had voluntarily assembled thus in batches to make it easy for them to be gathered to God. The managements of the eating-houses had scraped circles or triangles or squares or lunes in the frosted rear glass of their windows through which the prudent could observe the imprudent eating lime-green hens. Objects in breeches and skirts trod on the grey-green cellar lights and applauded themselves for their intrepidity. A girl with her partner passed by hurriedly; a shell-pink dance frock was showing below her dark coat. Suddenly she leaned forward and, egging her face onwards to a gambler's vivacity, said sweetly, "But Joseph . . ." Two workmen passed by; one of them was saying vehemently and gutturally, "Play yer cards, I said, play yer cards."

The albino had halted by the O'Connell Monument. His eyes were luminous in the dark.

"Hey!" called Lowe. "Whatta yeh doin'?"

Byrne did not answer. He stepped softly in under the statue where it was semi-dark. He ripped the slip-knot on the sack's mouth, caught the sack by the bottom, and spilled the hare out on the ground. The animal was

cramped: he gave three sorry hops, then crouched
against the base of the statue. Above him Octopus
O'Connell gave no indication of ambling.

(A hare is composed of three delightful ovals with
swivels at the neck and loins. First there is the great
oval of the body, balanced above and below by the
smaller ovals of the head and hind quarters. The oval of
the hind quarters is fragmentary but may be indicated
satisfactorily enough by a simple illustration. The flexible
ears are propellers, the tail a rudder. After that it is a
question of power propelling a mechanism that is in
perfect equipoise.

But wherever the power of the animal is generated,
it finds expression in the spatulate hind legs which have
the gift of spurning the world. Spurning the world—
that's the secret out! That is what makes the hare so
surpassingly gallant and his beholders so chagrined and
superstitious.)

Sallowface was very quiet as he watched the albino.
The tic flicked in his morose features. His face cleared
as he gradually acquitted his companion of black-
guardism. Byrne had begun to smile curiously; he
crouched with legs set well apart. His two palms began
to aim the hare towards the lighted street. The animal
moved in the desired direction but, as yet, his gait con-
sisted of despicable lopes. There was no indication that
he could be so transcendently swift. Suddenly he
stopped and began to cosy himself on a tram-track.
Then he looked like an illustration of a hare in a
child's picture-book. A breath of river-wind came upon
him and eddied his fur; this wind also edged the
albino's anger. He stripped his teeth and shouted, "Yeh-
Yeh-Yeh!" He raced his heavy boots and cried "Hulla-
hulla-hulla!" as he slipped his imaginary hounds. The
somnolent hare became suddenly charged with action.
First he sprang erect until he was a vibrant red loop
laced with white shadow. His ears were tubed to the

street. Then he began to pelt up mid-road. All the while the maniacal teeth of the albino were volleying "Yeh-Yeh-Yeh!" behind him.

At first the hare's passing occasioned little comment. The people continued to stilt along or stand in lack-lustre lumps. Then someone began to cry out "The Hare! The Hare!"

(You have seen the breeze impishly test the flexibility of a barley field; you have seen a child's hand ruffle the tassels of a countrywoman's shawl; you have seen a window-wind bring to life the dead hair of a deskful of schoolgirls.)

"The Hare! The Hare!"

Passion sprang up in the people as if it were a Jack-in-the-Box. The alert among the six thousand persons began to gesticulate and run. "The Hare! The Hare!" they shouted. The street rocked in its own uproar. The rushing, roaring people miraculously had sons and sisters and friends.

"The Hare! The Hare!"

Meanwhile the animate talisman darted here and there, setting his red torch to the golden thatch of the street. Now and again he stopped abruptly. When he did so, no part of the street was hidden from his exophthalmic-goitrous eyes. His ability to stop was amazing. There was no doubt whatseoever that he was terrified, yet his body was incapable of demonstrating dread and thus his terror masqueraded as alertness. He seemed to be aware that the milling people were roaring for his blood. And the people? They continued to demonstrate that mankind is a huge wind-rocked stone balanced on a cliff-face. Either that or (absurdity of absurdities) the greyhound is present in everyone, together with the bittern, the plaice, and the elephant.

Then the blazing galleon of a tram bore down upon the animal. He lost the sense of his exits. He raced towards the lighted street wall which miraculously opened before him in the form of an entrance to a subterranean barber's shop. He sped downwards, breaking the many parallel gleams of the metal stair-treads.

The barbers stood in reverent ranks attending to the customers. With long cool hops the hare passed through and went in the half-open doorway of an inner storeroom which was roofed at its farthest end by opaque cellar-lights. The room had a repulsive smell compounded of superannuated combs and hair-oil in semi-rusty tins. Along one wall was a long bench. The hare lay down beneath it.

The crowd from the street surged down the stairway. They were a shade intimidated when they saw the hieratic gestures of the barbers. The head barber came forward—he also owned the premises—and began to shepherd the intruders with his scissors and comb. His name was Richard Collis and he had the urbanity that has come to be associated with commercial competence. The man had a skull the shape of an inflated pig-bladder; his complexion, though a trifle over-scarlet, was undoubtedly first class. The points of his moustache were his twin-treasures and compensated in some measure for a childless marriage. His thinning hair was as a large cross placed on his bare shoulders. With every step he took towards the intruders he filched the significance from their entrance and made it appear a vulgar brawl.

"It's a hare, mister."

"A hare's after coming into your shop."

They took refuge in defeated laughter and the inevitable puns.

Richard Collis brought the full searchlight of his suavity to bear on the crowd on the stairway. Those nearest him were light-blinded by its rays. But his rear was unguarded: he felt the nick-snip of the many scissors die down behind him and whenever a snip did come it seemed as if one of the younger barbers were cocking a snook at his poll. He turned to his staff and rebuked them with a glance. The music of scissors and razor began again, but at a much slower tempo. Turning once more, he found the people at the head of the stairway quite merry and mutinous. It took all his charm and tact to expel them without appearing undignified.

Then a young barber pointed and said: "He's gone into the room, sir."

Richard Collis asked his customer to hold him excused. He entered the store-room, switched on the light and closed the door softly behind him. He saw the hare beneath the bench—a brown huddle which had achieved an unmistakable domesticity. The animal's panting was difficult to apprehend. Step by step the barber stole nearer. The hare swivelled his head but did not move away. Richard Collis got down on his knees. The hare watched him, first with friendliness, then with apathy. There came a sudden lull in the minor thunder of boots on the cellar lights. The barber stayed thus watching the hare for an appreciable while.

Then Richard Collis's countenance sagged, spruced, then sagged irretrievably. The skin of his face, as yet under some small control, proved to be covering a volatile squirming flesh. Unsuspected nerves jerked in patches like wind-flaws on still water. His tongue had ballooned and was filling his mouth. His lower lip essayed speech a few times before it succeeded.

"Wisha, God be with you, Ballintierna in the morning!"

He continued to kneel thus in trance while high in his mind the years clinked by like silver beads. Gradually his face grew less ruined. At last the renewed thunder of the boots on the cellar-glass aroused him. Then he arose and returned to his shop, closing the door reverently behind him.

A Woman's Hair

On Sunday afternoons when the bar was closed and my father had gone off to a football match my mother would take the opportunity offered by the quiet house to wash her beautiful hair. There were times when she would do so, I realized later, solely to gratify me, her only daughter—and indeed, her only child.

When my mother's hair was washed, rinsed and had almost dried, I would insist on her sitting on a rocking-chair. I would then stand on a chair beside her to catch the cascading hair above the point where it had gently tangled and would resolutely force the comb through it. As accurately as I recall the texture of my mother's hair, I also remember my stolid father's incomprehension of it as a bond between me and her: all he seemed to understand was the filling of spill-over pint glasses for the cartmen and countrymen who made the vacant lot at our gable on the town's edge a stopping-place on their way to the market.

But always between my mother and me, and complementary to the bond of flesh and blood, was the shining spancel of hair. I combed it and plaited it and piled it and experimented with it until my fat father, bustling in and out of the kitchen, scarcely knew whether to laugh or to scowl at such tomfoolery which—to him—was of a piece with my mother's obsession with music and the incomprehensible tock-tock of the metronome on the top of our piano. And when, as ladylike as she had lived, my mother died, I was left with the memory of her hair spread out like a fan on the white linen pillows on either side of her waxen face.

After my mother's death—I was then ten years of age—I was sent to a boarding school: I pined for home and after two months was brought back and packed off to the local convent day school, where I was an irregular attender, being kept at home on slight pretexts. At this time I was something of a day dreamer: washing ware at the window of the scullery, I would look out on to the vacant lot beside our house and watch the carters unyoke their horses and tie hissing nose-bags of oats about the animals' necks. I recall seeing a thunder shower fall on an unprotected box-cart of unslaked lime so that later the rocks of lime bubbled like molten lava. At certain times, too, the place grew still more interesting, for it was a halting-place for the restless of the Irish roads—umbrella-menders, ballad-singers, knife-grinders, men and women all subject to the compulsion and tyranny of movement.

One Saturday evening in early January as dusk fell, a tramp and his wife—more likely his "woman"—pitched a crude shelter just below our scullery window. The ice-cold air and the early evening stars had already given warning that a night of heavy frost would follow. The shelter was a crude one—a dirty canvas sheet slung over a ridge-pole held three feet above the ground by a few curved sally rods with limestones fallen from our yard wall to keep the soiled skirt of the camp in place. The shelter could be entered at either end, simply by groping back the flaps.

The tramp was black-bearded and was sixty if he was a day while the woman seemed to be in her early twenties. She had clear-cut features with a weather-worn complexion and there was in her stare a vacancy that seemed to offer a clue to such an odd pairing.

But it was her luxuriant dark hair that, despite its tangled and even filthy nature, attracted my attention. It appeared to be of a finer texture than my own hair, or indeed than that of my mother's, but the wind and sun had played havoc with it. I grimaced at the thought that such hair seemed a waste on the young woman's head.

As darkness fell, the tramp and his woman entered our bar, squatted on the floor in a corner, and began to drink stolidly, now and again muttering gutturally at each other. My father kept growling half-refusals to their requests for more drink, but the tramp and the woman kept blackmailing him and begging for more. I felt that my father continued to serve them simply because my mother had always pleaded for the "travellers": "Don't judge them, Tom—their life is hard. If they get drunk itself," she would say, "what harm is it? And they haven't far to go when they leave us—only from the bar to the gable outside."

So, aloof and alone, the oddly-matched pair drank and muttered and growled and lisped and never spared an upward glance for the other customers.

When closing time was called, and overcalled, the travelling pair, with my father hanging threateningly above them, at last staggered to their feet, bundled themselves out the door and moved towards their shelter, where, swaying giddily, they groped at the flaps and at last fumbled in and down, almost bringing the canvas about their ears with their blundering movements. Watching them from the darkness through the just-open window of the scullery, the night air icy on my face, I wondered at the mystery of the cave in which they slept, with perhaps their bodies oddly tangled in one another. Then I looked up at the frost polished heavens, shuddered in the night cold, and finally, closing the window without a sound, eased home the brass bolt on it. Thoughtfully I made my way to bed.

In the morning I awoke to find that the frost had painted palm-trees on the window-pane. I prepared the Sunday breakfast, then glanced out at the now glittering canvas of the tent. The frost had made the morning air soundless so that the town seemed unusually still. My father always slept out on Sunday mornings. As I came downstairs after having given him his breakfast in bed I heard a low knocking at the side-door.

I tiptoed out into the hallway. As again the knocking came, "Who's out?" I asked sharply. "Me!" said the deep hoarse voice which I recognised at once as being that of the bearded tramp. "What do you want?" I asked. "A knife—or a scissors," he growled. I paused, a constriction of fear in my heart. "My father is in bed," I told him. "Can you wait till he gets up?" "I must get it now—we have to be off!" The man's "We have to be off" assuaged my latent fear that he meant harm, yet I asked: "What do you want it for?" "Something that's caught in the frost!" "Is it the canvas?" "Give me a knife or a scissors and I'll return it safely," he muttered in reply.

I stood irresolute. A knife — no! But I could give him the battered black-and-silver tailor's scissors that was in the drawer of our kitchen table. With a cry of "Wait!" I ran, rattled open the drawer and going to the door, opened it cautiously and handed out the scissors. A glimpse told me that the man was sober but that his face was haggard and white-cold with traces of drink-rust about his lips. Muttering a word of thanks he moved away.

After a time, I ran to the scullery, climbed on a chair and, leaning over the sink, looked out at the shelter. What I saw made me cry out and beat with my knuckles on the frame of the window. I unshot the bolt, swung open the window on its hinges and screamed "No! No!" at the top of my voice.

The tramp, who was kneeling on the ground at one end of the shelter, looked upwards over his shoulder at me. His black hat was pitched high on his head and a single lock of hair was plastered onto his white sweating forehead. "No! No!" I screamed again, then leaping off the chair, I raced through the kitchen, tore into the shop, grabbed a claw-hammer from the tool-box under the counter and, opening the hall door, went pelting out.

The man, tne scissors still in his hands, was on
one knee at the end of the tent. Beneath him,
prone on the ground and protruding from under
the canvas of the shelter, lay the woman's head and
breast. The tumult of her hair was spread out beneath
her head. I verified what I had guessed at from my first
glimpse through the window, that her hair was frost-
locked in a small but comparatively deep pool of water
that lay just outside the end of the camp and that the
tramp was about to cut the hair so as to release it. The
woman's face could have been the one carved in cameo
on the brooch my mother wore, but for the fact that the
rust of old drink befouled her lips about which an odd
not-caring smile now played. The white skin of her lower
throat and upper breasts was in startling contrast to
her dark complexion and to the soiled ground beneath
her head. "Wait!" I cried again, pushing the man aside;
crouching, my fingers verified that the hair was gripped
in a frozen pool of animal urine.

I tilted the head sideways and, with the hammer-head,
began to hack at the edge of the frozen pool. Under my
blows the ice cracked brown-white at its edges. When
I had reduced part of the edge of the pool to powder, I
tried with the claw of the hammer to lever upwards on
the ragged iceblock of the frozen pool. Try as I would
I failed to gain purchase on the ravelling ice.

The man, still in a kind of animal crouch, was directly
behind me and watching me dully. He still held the
scissors in his hand. Again I attacked, seemingly as fruit-
lessly as before, for even the claw of the hammer could
do little more than break off futile smithereens. Although
I continued to pound and claw, releasing the hair seemed
a baffling task.

I paused; then furious and tense, I snatched the
scissors from the man's hand. Forcing its two points together to make a single point which I thrust deep under
the iceblock, I began to lever the ice upwards. At first

I made no impression on it but, at last, hearing the ice
squeak, I again inserted the scissors at a different
place, this time with its points about an inch apart and
then, levering with all my strength, brought the whole
irregular frozen block in which the spread of the
woman's hair was locked, completely free of the ground.

For a moment or two, utterly spent, I hung above the
woman; then I half-dragged, half-helped her to her feet
where, smiling grotesquely she continued to regard me
sidelong with slightly daft, slightly whimsical, wholly
animal eyes. Her neck and shoulders were white and bare
and the brown dripping block of ice dangled between
her shoulder blades.

Gripping the hammer and scissors I began to push
her out into the street and towards our hall-door which
still stood ajar. I pushed her into the kitchen where
by now the morning range was a grin of fire. Sobbing
somewhat, I steered her before me into the scullery.
There, standing on a chair, I made her bow her neck
as I filled an enamel basin with hot water. Cupping the
water in my hands I began to pour it over the matted
poll. I kept working furiously until the melting ice began
to fall in chunks into the basin. Then I took up a bar
of soap and began frenziedly to lather the woman's
hair. I found myself working under an odd compulsion.

Not a word passed between us. Again and again I
changed the water in the basin until at last as I rinsed
the hair, the water poured clearly. I piled a bath-towel
about the woman's head, rubbed furiously for some time,
and then folding and turning the towel I piled it turban-
wise about her head.

She watched dreamily as I took a large oval-shaped
zinc bathtub and, setting it on the floor, affixed a length
of hose to the nozzle of the hot-water tap and sent
steaming water pouring into the vessel. Almost stamp-
ing my foot I indicated to the woman that she should
stand into the vessel and wash herself. Dully she began

to drop her rags to the floor: I tip-toed upstairs and, opening the mahogany wardrobe on the landing, piled a skirt and blouse of my dead mother over one arm and later snatched some underclothes from a drawer beside it. A pair of lizard-skin shoes, old fishnet stockings these too I took; then, finally, opening a dusty trunk I took out a clutch of hairpins and a fancy comb inset with brilliants.

Returning to the kitchen, I peeped through the keyhole into the scullery; the woman was still standing in the steaming tub, indolently rubbing the cake of soap to her limbs. Young as I was, I realized that she had a beautiful body.

I prepared the breakfast: when I thought that she had finished washing herself I pushed open the door a little and left the clothes on the floor inside it. After a time I heard the basin clank against the trough and the scrape of the woman's nails as she rinsed the vessel. A little while later she came slowly out, wearing my mother's clothes.

Holding my breath I watched her walk forward. The house was without sound. In mid-kitchen she turned and, looking at the table, indicated that she wished to eat. I placed food before her. She ate her breakfast slowly and thoughtfully, crumbs falling unheeded to the floor. When she had finished, I placed the delf on a tray and then pointed to the rocking-chair by the fire. The woman rose slowly, went and sat on it. I took the tray to the scullery, piled the ware into a basin, ran the hot water on it and then returned to the kitchen. From a press to the left of the fire I took a strong-toothed comb and standing behind the woman, unwound the turban and set about combing out the drying hair.

I was patient with the hair, teasing it gently where it had knotted and working diligently until at last it was a blue-black thunder-cloud about her head and shoulders. Between me and the glow of the fire its edges were rimmed with red-gold. Wholly absorbed, I kept on combing as the hair became drier and more beautiful—more tractable too, until at last it glistened and shone and shook and floated and fell in plenitude about her waist. The woman turned her head quite sensitively to accommodate me as I worked.

At last I combed the hair back over the woman's ears and, setting aside the comb, began to plait and pile it, twisting it this way and that, pinning it at a point that took my fancy by inserting the comb with the brilliants in it and then undoing it capriciously as if dissatisfied with the result. The hair, now wholly dry, was sensual under my fingers, so that I was reluctant to finish, and time and again with an exclamation of sham annoyance, I let the piled hair fall. Each time I broke off, the woman smiled at my feigned disappointment. About us the house grew still more silent.

This went on for some time until I could find no excuse for continuing. Then the woman's long bare arm curled intuitively about me and drew me gently down on to her lap. At first I was inclined to resist, but her implied certainty that I would obey her was so absolute that I yielded. There was a pause in which my buttocks tested the welcome seat offered by her thighs, then, reassured, I sent my arm over her shoulder and dug my fingers deep into the thicket of hair at the nape of her neck.

Almost imperceptibly at first, but with a mounting sense of rhythm, and muttering, humming and crooning as she moved, the woman began to rock backwards and forwards on the chair with a movement reminiscent of the metronome on the piano-top. I found myself nestling closer to her breasts: of its own volition my head butted intuitively against her and before I knew, or cared, my lips and teeth were on her nipples. I heard myself as at a distance mouthing warm pleasant incoherencies.

So drugged were we both that the vague knocking on

the hall door did not disturb us: nor a moment or two later did the sight of my father in the kitchen doorway dressed only in his pants and shirt, with the bearded tramp standing beside him, trouble us in the least. After an uncomprehending glance at us the two men turned away and moved dully into the bar leaving us alone to rock out a solution to one of the many compulsions of our shared womanhood.

Evening in Ireland

The mountains were thrown higgledy-piggledy into the distance where the sea was. The white dusty road wound around the near flank of the valley and then fell gracefully away to the one-arched bridge below. Among the few tufted oaks beyond the bridge the church lurked. A cluster of thatched houses crouched about it. Bird song had shrivelled and died.

The old priest came down the road. He was walking slowly. He was a sandy-grey man with lush eyebrows. His lips moved in prayer as his eyes found and lost the words in the breviary. From time to time his eyes wandered over the breviary and over the spectacles down the long curve of the white road.

A young man came upwards from the bridge. On his back he carried a sack. There was a hole in the sack through which a turkey's head protruded into the sunlight. The priest squeezed up his eyes and saw the man clearly. At the same time the young man spied the priest. He ceased his whistling and threw aside his slouch. He jerked the sack one notch higher on his shoulder. He crossed to the road margin opposite to that on which the priest was walking. The priest and the man came closer to one another. The man pulled the visor of his cap down over his eyes and tried to sneak past. Unaccountably the priest was on the road before him. The young man tipped his cap with a forefinger. He mumbled something.

The priest screwed up his face a few times. This was designed to wring the sun out of his features. Also to intimidate the young man. The priest said, with a soft harshness: 'Who have I?'

'Dick Lynch, Father.'

'Are you a son of Dick the River or of Dick the White Stile?'

'Dick the River, Father.'

'What have you in the sack?'

'A turkey hen, Father.'

'Where are you taking her?'

A pause. A glint. A sudden spurt of brave speech. 'To the cock, Father.'

The priest eyed the young man narrowly. The young man held his face to a sterling gravity as the priest walked all around him. The turkey hen and the priest looked at one another. The bird closed her eyes so that they were two white discs. She seemed grotesquely to be mimicking a sleeping doll.

The priest returned and faced the young man. 'H'm!' he said. Then: 'Are you married?'

'No, Father.'

'I wouldn't doubt you! How many in family are ye?'

'Six, Father.'

'What way are ye divided?'

'Four girls and two boys, Father.'

'Are the girls older or younger than you?'

'The three eldest are girls, Father. The last girl is younger than me.'

'Any of them married?'

'No, Father.'

'Tck! Tck! Tck! That's right! Mate yeer turkeys and lie fallow yeerselves. Keep on that way, let ye, until ye're tall grey curmudgeons fit for nothing else but to stone a braddy cow out of a garden. Is it blind ye are? Will ye look at the world teeming with fertility?'

Dutifully the young man eyed the fertile world.

'Did you ever hear what the Almighty God said to Adam and Eve?'

'I forget, Father.'

'You wouldn't forget the ballad of "Big Mick's Cow"! What kind of people are ye at all? Do ye want to have me, or the man that comes after me here, parsing the parables to the red varnish of the pews or talking to himself about the road from Jericho to Jerusalem? Ay! and the thatch mouldering on the roofs around the house of God.' A pause for breath. Then: 'Your eldest sister —what name have ye on her?'

'Pidge, Father.'

'Is she the one that has the black hair like this?' The priest made a gesture indicative of unusual coiffure.

'Yes, Father.'

'She's shoving on into years, isn't she?'

'She is, Father.'

'She'll never see thirty again?'

'She won't, Father.'

'Is she keeping company with anyone?'

'Not to my knowledge, Father.'

'H'm! Do you know Denis Sullivan of Parkeen?'

'Denisheen the Dog, is it, Father?'

'Dog! Dog! Dog! What dog, man?'

'He have a dog, Father, a black and white dog.'

'I'm asking if you know him?'

'I do, Father.'

'Nine cows he has?'

'Yes, Father.'

'Lovely ground. In good heart. Tucks of running water.'

'Ay, Father.'

'Enough fowl to blacken the air?'

'Yes, Father.'

'A tub trap and a roan pony?'

'He has so, Father.'

'And a Department bull?'

The farmer became paramount in the young man. 'Let me tell you something, Father. That same bull is gettin' poorly. He's throwing the world and all of white calves.'

The priest bridled up. 'And what signifies that? Won't a postage stamp and a small bit of writing swap him? When he's transferred won't some other parish beside ours breed the pale delicate cattle? Answer me out!'

Meekly, conquered: 'That's true, Father.'

'Come now, wouldn't Denisheen the Dog, as you call him, suit your sister, Pidge?'

'He might, Father.'

'Wouldn't you do an act of charity and put it into her head?'

The young man remained silent.

'Will you tell it to your father, itself?'

'I will indeed, Father.'

'Tell him to be doing his duty by ye, will you?'

'I will, Father.'

'Tell him that I said if he doesn't look after ye, who will?'

'That's right, Father.'

'That's right! That's right! That's right!' the priest said peevishly. 'Can ye do anything but agree with me?'

After a moment of irresolute silence, he said brightly: 'There's a spark in you. You showed it when you denounced the bull.'

The young man smiled under the peak of his cap. The hen turkey made a noise that sounded like: *'Pewtk!'*

The priest said: 'Were you at Conway's, the gathering-house, on Wednesday night?'

Reluctantly: 'I was, Father.'

'Inside or out?'

'Mostly outside, Father.'

'Had ye a raffle?'

'There was a raffle, Father, but I was gone home.'

'Oho, you were, you model! H'm! What music had ye?'

'I couldn't get a glimpse of the musicianers, Father. I'd say it was a pair from away up Reesk direction.'

Silence. The two men looked at one another.

The priest's mouth was giving him a great deal of trouble. All the while his eyes transfixed and intimidated the young man. When he had gained the mastery over his lips he said in a low voice: 'Goodbye, son!'

The young man strode steadily up the road. After 'Goodbye, Father!'

The young man strode steadily up the road. After moving uphill for a little distance he turned his head quickly. His mouth was fully open in rustic laughter. But he was caught red-handed, for the priest, too, had turned and was standing quietly, looking at him over his glasses.

The young man wiped the smile from his face.

'Come back here!' the priest said sternly.

Embarrassed, Dick Lynch shuffled back.

'Ha!' the priest began. 'Making game of your pastor, you are! What's in your mind is written plainly on your face. Isn't that a nice carry-on for a Sunday evening?'

The young man shifted his weight from one boot to the other.

The priest was relentless. 'I know you, me hayro!' he said. He began to mimic himself and the boy:

'What have you in the sack, son?'

'A turkey-hen, Father.'

'And where are you taking her?'

'To the cock, Father.'

The priest's voice was poised between banter and reproof. Then, his mimicry finished, he said: 'You'll swing, you scoundrel, won't you?'

'I will, Father.' Dick Lynch for good measure of agreement added a small smile, which the priest straightaway guillotined.

'Pewtk!' said the turkey.

Again the priest was at the mimicry. *'I will, Father! I will, Father!'* His voice climbed. 'Now, a fair warning I'm giving you. You know my old housekeeper?'

'I do, Father.'

'Her sight is going and her wits are wandering. But her hearing is unimpaired. She hears the grass growing in this parish.' The priest's voice was threatening: 'I'm giving you timely notice. If 'tis a thing she brings home a funny story about myself and a turkey-hen, I'll, I'll ...'

A remote look on the young man's face made the priest

turn to follow the other's gaze. Down on the bridge in the valley he saw what the young man was looking at with such intensity: a tall heavily-built man and a young red-haired girl. The man was walking slightly behind the girl and was talking over her shoulder. Whatever it was he was saying was sending her off into peals of young laughter. Now and again the girl swung away from the heavy man, but always she returned to him as if controlled by a strong elastic band.

'Who's he?' asked the priest. The tone of his voice implied that he and the young man were conspirators.

The young man was silent. He looked over-long at the pair on the bridge. Quietly he said: 'Meehan, Father.'

'Ho-ho!' said the priest. 'Meehan, the Prince of Philanderers! Into God's net the rascal is cast. You know him, don't you?'

Evenly: 'I've heard tell of him, Father.'

'Of course you have! The stones of the road have heard of his prowess as a philanderer. First he was going with a daughter of Rory Gibbons; then it was that jet-black daughter of Mike McLoughlin of Creveen he was walking out. And after that he knocked a turn out of the young widow-woman who has a public house at Baurscoob Cross-roads. What's this her name is, son?'

'Mrs. Hanafin, Father.'

'Ay! That's it! Who's the lassie with him now?'

'Mary Teresa O'Donnell, Father.'

The priest looked sharply at the young man. His age had suddenly been sloughed. Now he was sharper than sharp. 'Tell me,' he said, as if inserting a knife-blade into a crevice, 'this Mary Teresa O'Donnell, was she at the gathering-house on Wednesday?'

'She was, Father.'

'Did you dance with her?'

'I did, Father.'

'You danced with no one else?'

'No, Father.' The young man was replying as from a

trance.

'Tell me, son, did you convey her home?'

'No, Father.'

'Did she go home with Meehan?'

Over-sharply the young man said: 'It's no business of mine who she went home with.'

The priest and the young man fell silent. They stood watching the antics of the pair below them. Then the boy turned bitterly and made as if to walk away uphill. The priest called to him softly.

'A question I want to ask you,' he said. 'I'm going on down there. I'll be meeting Meehan. Yes or no, son, will I roast him?'

'That's up to yourself, Father.'

'It's not up to myself! It's up to you, only that a foolish honour has you throttled. Now, now, no hole-and-corner play! As a representative of the Almighty God, I'm asking you a straight question. Soon I'll be on the bridge. It's easy for me to pass Meehan by with a civil dodderin' word. It's just as easy for me to do the other thing. For the last time, yes or no, will I roast Meehan the Philanderer? He's wily: you're young. The odds are against you. As play goes, it's fair enough!'

The boy looked down. He was tempted. His lips and eyes were taken with whimsy, then with a smiling hardness.

'You might as well, Father,' he said softly.

'Do you think that I have it in me to roast him?'

The smile became a true laugh. 'Certain sure I am of it, Father.'

'Right! Now suppose I redden and grill Meehan, will you play square with this O'Donnell girl?'

In a low voice: 'I will, Father.'

'You've thought the matter over?'

'I've thought of little else, Father.'

'There'll be none of this Kathleen Mavourneen courtship—it may be for years and it may be for ever?'

'No, Father.'

'No putting of the holy day on the long finger?'

'No, Father.'

'The money question, is that settled?'

A gush of talk from the young man. 'That was threshed out between us, Father. There's no difficulty there. I have three hundred pounds in dry cash in my own name. She has seven hundred pounds coming to her. Cahillane's holding is on the walls. 'Twill be bought for seven hundred and fifty. What's left will stock the land.'

'That's settled so, son?'

'Settled it is, Father.'

'You'll give me your word?'

'My word, Father!'

'God bless you, son.'

'And you, Father.'

The young man turned, hitched his sack higher on his back and strode uphill to mate the turkey. The priest braced himself and strode downhill to mate the young man. The heavy sun slid down the heavens to where the mountains waited in the far west. Striding freely into the upland, the young man laughed. He had just thought of what God had said to Adam and Eve. How could he have forgotten it? It was: 'Go forth, increase and multiply, and fill the earth.'

The Sound of the Bell

Sunday Mass was over, and the priest was removing his vestments when there was a rap on the heavy sacristy door. Maurice Fitz, the old parish clerk, opened it. Outside he saw a cluster of men, mostly middle-aged and old. The clerk's eyes narrowed. 'Oh, the little dabchicks,' he said, 'the little dabchicks from Boherbeg.'

'We want to see the parish priest,' said one of the men, a tall hook-nosed fellow, wearing riding breeches and leggings.

'If you do, Mister Gravel Pit, you'll have to wait till he's finished his thanksgiving.'

'We'll wait!'

The clerk closed the door slowly, narrowly eyeing the the men as he did so. He was dressed in greeny-black cloth. Jutting into the nape of his stiff collar were the icicles of his poor grey hair. When he was left with but a small aperture through which to peer, he said: 'Riddle-me-riddle-me-ree! Boots and breeding brought them here.' His astonishingly sensible face redeemed the eccentricity of this statement.

The ten or eleven men waited under the damp inhospitable stone of the church. Every man, except the man with the riding-breeches, had his right shoulder higher than his left. This was from constant use of spade and slawn. One man stood a little to the rear. He was dumpy and his face was dyed purple by the cold. A drop of water at the end of his long nose made him look extremely disconsolate. His attitude indicated a vague desire to be disassociated from the others. The man with the riding-breeches thrust his hands deep into his fob pockets and looked around in order to stiffen the loyalty him and said timidly: 'Maybe 'twould be better to call of the others. The man with the purple face glanced at to see him in the house to-morrow, Richie?'

'We'll see him here and now!' said the other stoutly.

Just then the door opened — seemingly of its own volition — and the men trooped in.

Father Fennell was drying his hands on a linen towel. He was less a tiny man than a large man shrunken. He seemed frail and defenceless. He had a habit of blinking. As he dried his hands he looked down at the big boots moving across the polished parquetry. The men had now formed a solid ring around him. The clerk slammed the door with unnecessary loudness and scampered around the periphery of the ring until he was near the priest. He took a brass candlestick from a table. His movements implied a distrust of the men's honesty.

'Good day, men,' said the priest.

'Good day, Father Fennell,' chorused the men.

The man with the purple face was now in front. 'Hard weather for this time of year, Father . . . .'

'Is that you, Johnny Mahoon? Well? Any word from Jim?'

Johnny Mahoon inflated. 'Next time he'll come home he'll have the collar, Father.'

'With the help of God, Johnny!' said the priest.

'With the help of God, Father,' said Johnny with meekness and pride.

There was a lull. The clerk opened a wardrobe door and discommoded some of the deputation. He thrust his head in among the bright vestments and began to sing: *'Who'll hang the ringer on the black cat's neck? Who'll hang the ringer on the black cat's neck?'*

The heavy boots stirred uneasily.

The priest balled up the towel and dropped it on a small table. 'Well, men, what brought ye?' he asked.

The men looked at Richie MacNamara of the gravel pit. Out of his fob pockets Richie's hands seemed unsure and nervous. Nevertheless, he began: 'We came, Father, about the bell!'

'The bell?'

'Ay! the new bell!'

'What about it? A little high-pitched in tone, but just the same everybody says 'tis a grand bell.'

A deep voice came from among the men: 'It's a fine bell for them that are living in the shadow of the steeple.'

'Wax!' said the parish clerk.

'I don't quite follow ye,' said Father Fennell.

Richie MacNamara had become brave: 'You put a shilling a cow on us to pay for that bell. At Donovan's station—you, remember, Father?'

'I remember. And ye paid it like good Christian men.'

'Wax!' said the parish clerk.

'Father,' Richie enquired, 'did any man from Boherbeg ever default in his station money?'

'Not in my time!'

'No, Father! Nor in Father Gibson's time! Nor in Father Prendiville's time! Nor in Father Danny O'Shea's time! Nor in the time of any parish priest that came before you. And another thing, Father, did we ever deny you your lawful Christmas dues?

'Ye did not!'

'And did we ever leave you short of the winter's firing?'

'Never! That goes without saying.'

'And we paid our part for the new bell, didn't we?'

'Ye did. Ye did. Ye did.'

The clerk was opening and slamming drawers. '*Around the world for sport,*' he sang: '*around the world for sport.*'

Richie MacNamara turned. 'We were talking to the parish priest,' he said, 'and not to the parish clerk.' He made the word clerk sound like an obscenity.

The old man straightened himself. He swivelled deliberately, wet his lips with a meditative tongue, narrowed his eyes and said: 'Richie MacNamara, I remember the morning you were christened. An ugly little scaldie with ropes of black hair on you and the bubble in your skull moving in and out.' He snorted. 'They must ha' been damn fond o' children when they r'ared you.'

Richie MacNamara reddened. The priest raised a pacifying hand. Johnny Mahoon stepped into the breach. Since his son was going for the Church he reckoned that he had a leg in both worlds.

'Father, about that bell! We gave it a fair trial. We tested it from all angles and airts and in all winds and weathers. And it's our contention that the bell can't be heard beyond Teerfeeney Cross.'

The clerk stopped folding a maniple to snort: 'It can be heard in Moinveenagh and in Derrigo. It can even be heard in Clounassig with a hill between. 'Tis a queer state of affairs that it should skip the holy hollow of Boherbeg.'

Johnny Mahoon refused to be deflected. 'We couldn't fault th' ould bell, Father. We set our clocks to it. We began and ended work to it. The wimmin put down the praties to it and we came back from the bog to it. If it was a thing it was a dead bell we said a Lord-ha'-mercy on the soul of the faithful departed. If 'twas a Mass bell we took care to be in good time. And if it was a thing it rang out in the heart of the night, we knew that something terrible had happened . . . that there was a fire, or . . . .'

'. . . that the parish priest had died,' said the sepulchral voice somewhere in the deputation.

'God spoke first!' said the clerk sharply, implying that Father Fennell might bury the lot of them.

Richie MacNamara brought his face close to the priest's. 'We never went ag'in a parish priest yet!' he half-threatened.

The clerk guffawed and slammed home a drawer. 'Oho, ye did not!' he said. 'Except the time of the pews! And the time of the wran-dance! And the time of the raffle for the half-a-cow!'

'Bridle your tongue, man!' Father Fennell ordered his clerk.

The clerk took a conical candle-extinguisher from the wall and opened the door leading to the sanctuary. He turned. 'What did Father Gibson call ye? The pagans of the parish, with yeer eggs in one another's hay-wynds and yeer knots for ripping calves' guts and yeer three drops of cock's blood on the ace of hearts.'

The clerk clutched the extinguisher as if it were a lance. He raised his voice a full tone: 'And ye were never crowned till Father Prendiville called Boherbeg the boondoon of Ireland. Riddle-me-riddle-me-ree! Ye never wint ag'in a parish priest! What about the battle of the Red Gullet when the wounded shoemaker was cured with Ippo wine and squills?'

He slammed the door with a great hollow sound. The priest turned to the men. 'When he isn't a duke, he's a weasel. Ye haven't to put up with him the round of the year like I have. May God look down on me! I was a happy man in Ballytarv.' The deputation made belligerent noises of commiseration.

'About the bell,' continued the priest evenly: 'it was put there to be heard.'

'You took the word out of my mouth, Father,' said Johnny Mahoon.

'I'll tell ye what! I'll ramble up there one of these days to hear the midday Angelus. Wouldn't that be the best thing I could do?'

'That'll suit us gallant, Father,' chorused the men. 'Any day you name, Father. 'Tis a slack time o' the year.'

'Well, we'll say Tuesday; that is if his lordship will consent to drive the pony to Boherbeg.'

Johnny Mahoon was alert to change the subject. ' 'Twill go to the rain, Father,' he observed.

Judiciously: 'I wouldn't agree with you, Johnny.'

With sham concern: 'Wouldn't you now, Father?'

'No, John. The glass is steady. I'd say 'twould keep

up out of his coat. His head had the precise movements of a ventriloquist's doll. Watches flashed in and out among the old men to offset this distraction. Already the children were deserting. Richie MacNamara of the gravel pit came forward.

'I'd say it has the hour well spoiled now, Father,' he said severely.

Glowing with pleasure, the priest was watching a pointer fanning strongly on the upper ridge. 'Ha, ha!' he said. 'There's a game I served my time to.'

The dog, moving in his well-loved element, came down toward the people. Then the fowler broke the skyline. He stood for a little space and looked down at the scene below him. When the priest had risen from the chair, the fowler saw the cushion blaze up among the dark press of bodies. He made as if to move away but the cautious movements of his dog attracted him and he came gingerly onward. He was a tall man with a free stride. The pointer leaped from the turf-bank and nosed in the low ground. The people watched it working forward. The fowler descended through a gap in the bank.

Then the people of Boherbeg discovered that their priest had escaped.

The fowler stood waiting for Father Fennell, who was now approaching him with the stride of a boy. The dog slowed before a clump of rushes, then froze in dead set and gently raised its right paw. The priest took the gun from the fowler and stole up on the dog. Turn and turn about the dog was taut and quivering. The priest stooped and raised the gun to his shoulder. In this attitude he wasn't as big as a hatching hen. The ring of people prepared to receive the shot in their western ears.

Then from the east came the sound of the bell. 'Pling! Pling! Pling!' it went unmistakably. The priest wearily lowered the gun from his shoulder and turned a shrewd affectionate face on the people. The dog broke discipline and moved in on the game. The snipe rose and flung itself deftly at the air. With rusty squeakings it was exalted in the sky where it mimicked the blinkings of a skylark.

The clerk popped something into his mouth, grimaced wryly and said: 'This is a noble locality for sloes.'

By the Sea

Once on the gravelled path of the village the Boy Scouts squinted up at the bus-top. But the summer sun was a sudden splash of limewash in their eyes and their screwed faces faltered and fell. Down the broken gapped village street drove a wind tinctured with the sea, and immediately the boys began to laugh and twitter and twinkle like a flock of sparrows bathing in a deep well of road-dust.

Canvas, poles, tinware utensils, rucksacks and boxes came perilously down from the bus-top. Little hands clawed chattels safely home. Finally, all the gear was piled on the pathway; the conductor offered them his absolutely final company smile; a woman in the rear seat of the bus fisted a clear circle in the glass; the exhaust jetted blue-purple and the bus churned away. It left a huddle of blue-clad boys tangled in a medley of mostly green gear.

They trudged up to the higher end of the village. When they saw the sea they cheered. Between them and the sea, the sandhills below the village held creamy flanks lipped with generous shocks of emerald bent-grass. Out on the ocean there were no waves. There was little sound except the half-imagined, half-audible whisper of the inshore ripples, repeating "Lipsss, lipsss." To the right were the sun-drenched cliffs; to the left, the long, attenuating scimitar of red sand. From their place of vantage at the end of the village the boys halted to appreciate the sea, the squirming and crawling of it, the slithering and sidling of it, the terror and delight of it. Capricious highways of green ink wandered in its spurious blueness. Under a short cliff to the right floated a dirty blanket of unmoving foam which seemed independent of submarine movement. The sun, swinging pon-

derously above the cloudy mountain camps across the
bay, threw its royal image along the sea even to the
strand below. Seeing, hearing, smelling, tasting and
touching became luxuries. Luxuries, indeed, since there
was nothing worth seeing but the sea; nothing worth
hearing but the soft inshore "Lipsss, lipsss"; nothing
worth smelling or tasting but that which came to nostrils
and palate in wild salinity; nothing fit for the body's
touch but the velvet stroking of the waves.

Christy Hickey roused them. They turned from the
sea and dragged themselves up to the Castle gates: the
gates were set in a high corner of the green above the
ocean. Over the gapped demesne wall they saw the great
hulk of the burned building — its battlements cut
clearly out of the cooler northern sky. To the right of
the Castle they noticed the wing which had not suffered
in the conflagration — its doors and windows and
verandah shone very white in the sunlight. The boys
began to marvel at the gateway —they had never seen
such a gateway before. It was actually a dwelling-house,
and out of this fairy-tale portal walked a fairy-tale old
woman to laugh with them and at them, to welcome
them and to wonder at them, to feel the texture of the
blue cloth on their tunics, to finger their golden-coloured
crosses, and now and again to stoop to discover what
particular sample of sweating imp lurked beneath the
blue toadstool of a hat. The old lady caught Christy
Hickey's hand and showed no eagerness to release it as
she talked of soda-bread and butter-scotch and mush-
rooms on the coals, and eggs as brown as . . . as brown
as . . . here she tried heaven and earth and ocean for a
suitable comparison and failed to find one. When at last
the astonished youngsters estimated that there was a
period to her clucking, she began her incoherencies over
again just to show her delight at this, her new family.
Afterwards the white gates that showed blotches of rust
screamed open: the boys began to shout, "Where?

Where?" and to answer, "Over there! Over there!" They streamed across the grassy lawn and dumped their possessions beside the wall adjoining the road. Beyond the road was a short field that sloped down to a cliff above the sea. Above them the field lifted in gentle acclivity to the Castle. Below them stretched the fine span of the bay.

Bell-tents and bivouacs up, latrines, grease-traps and hip-hollows dug, flag hoisted; water-carriers, couriers and cooks appointed — all the dismal chores performed with new zest. The owner of the Castle came down to greet them. He was enormous, Irish, and friendly. He stood smiling at this ant-hill of activity on his land. He asked the Scoutmaster to bring the boys up to help him pick his gooseberries. He had many things that would interest them, he said.

The rest of the day was a great rush hither and thither in an effort to experience everything at the same time. They swam before dinner; after the swim they rushed here and there on the long strand marvelling at new wonders. They found three green glass balls and some huge chunks of cork. Also a battered wickerwork lobster pot. They walked along the tide's lip for the most of a mile and found things eloquent of the sea's mystery. On the high-water mark, clothed in seaweed, they saw the body of a marmoset — at least Jimmy Stephens said it was a marmoset, though the others considered it a plain monkey. Then there was the skeleton of what someone suggested was a bottle-nosed shark.

On the way back to the Castle they met the old parish priest—he examined them unbelievingly over his breviary before he addressed them. One of the younger Scouts stood on his hands to amuse the old man: the boy held his balance for a short time before sprawling backwards into the fuchsia. When they went up to the Castle they found marvel piled on marvel. The gooseberries were of two kinds, the red and hairy, and the amber and hairless.

The man who owned the Castle had a trick gooseberry. It was as big as a small apple. He had grown it by removing all but one of the immature fruits on a branch. By allowing this single gooseberry to droop into a cup of water he had produced a freak fruit. He also had a hawk chained to a perch: when the youngsters threw pieces of stick to it the bird pounced on them ferociously. There was a fig tree growing in the open air near the garden door. As a final titbit their host made his Alsatian leap high to pull a bell-rope. Towards evening, with bulging pockets, the Scouts ambled down the lawn.

Night came upon the Scouts and heightened their sense of adventure. True, they sang around the fire, more to justify a cardinal principle in Scout literature than from motives of inward urgency, but they were more than satisfied with this simulacrum of enjoyment—they enjoyed the singing and the firelight because it would be a type of blasphemy to admit that they did not enjoy it. But the strongest perceptible emotion amongst the boys was a type of inarticulate fear which the lusty singing did its share to dispel. Afterwards a great beast of a moon clambered up the blue velvet sky — the boys struggled to the top of the mossy wall and saw what wonders it could work on the ballroom floor of the ocean. As the daylight seeped out of the heavens the reiterated complaint of the tide-edge impinged more and more upon the conscious ear. Insignificant sounds increased in portentousness; the violent bugling of a cow from the shelter belt behind the Castle rocked the world; a spurt of laughter from the village almost approximated to rifle fire; a light flickering on the hills was a thing of great mystery. The boys crowded in on the dying fire. What remnants of cold the summer night held fastened its hooks in their backs. Christy Hickey watched them narrowly and was quick to recognize the sense of dwarfishness in their faces. The boys continued to shrill loudly in order to compensate for their inner cowardice.

Then the camp bugler stood up beyond the firelight and sounded "Taps". His instrument flung the separate notes out into the shining night sea. On leaving the bugle each note seemed to become a small silver globe that went bounding beautifully out to seek its fortune in a blue world. When he had finished, the echo of the music took a while to die.

Christy Hickey opened the end wall of his own white sleeping-tent and hung a large black crucifix within on the pole of the opposite tent-wall. Under the crucifix he suspended a lighting storm lantern. As he did so, he kept repeating softly to himself, "The tents of Israel, the tents of Israel." The boys crowded in on the mouth of the white tent, the surplus spilling out into the grassy bank. Then the Scoutmaster knelt beneath the crucifix and recited the Rosary. Prayers never seemed so delightful before; all the old appellations flashed new lights from unsuspected facets of grandeur. The praying fused them warmly into one another, as if indeed this single act of communal moonlight prayer had the power to make them blood brothers. The drone of the praying made them sleepy, too; when the Rosary and Litany were ended each small head was fully loaded with sleep.

Eight boys in each bell-tent—seven and a patrol leader. Christy Hickey and Jimmy Stephens were to sleep in the white sleeping-tent. Christy walked around, warning the boys not to put their hand to the canvas if it rained and impressing on the patrol leaders the necessity for loosening the guy ropes in a shower. Before long he blew the whistle for lights out. Afterwards he stayed at the wall for a while. He was looking out over the sea. He released breath through his nostrils in easy hisses of satisfaction. Now that the boys had retired and were safe, he found the knapsack of responsibility slipping from his shoulders. This was his first outing of this nature since his appointment as Scoutmaster, and, as the group was a new one, all but two of the boys had never been under canvas before. He looked across his shoulder. Just then Jimmy Stephens put his head out of the sleeping-tent that he and the Scoutmaster were to share, and looked expectantly towards the figure by the moonlit wall. Christy padded softly around the bell-tents. A snatch of eager narrative filtered through the canvas—". . . a weeny rabbit that a weasel killed—an', man, he was hot!" He walked to the triangular doors of the tents and threw back the canvas so as to give the boys air. Within, the boys were lying like the spokes of a wheel, the recumbent bodies radiating from the tent-pole. As he rustled away he found the dammed-up tittering break softly behind him. He smiled contentedly at the sound. Then he blessed himself, slipped into the tent and stripped speedily. Jimmy Stephens and himself conversed softly for a while before they bade each other good night.

Christy found it difficult to sleep. The excitement of the day, more or less dormant during dusk, now began to gnaw in him as a wary mouse gnaws in a house that has grown silent. Tittering began in one of the tents— the patrol leader's voice was raised in muffled reproval. An inquisitive cow began to lumber down the lawn. With his ear to the ground Christy could hear the animal tearing at the grass as if it were paper. The noise became more determined as the cow approached the tent. Finally the animal's shadow lunged across the canvas. He could hear her breathing and snuffling close to his face but he made no movement; he tautened his body and hoped that she would not become entangled in the tent-ropes. Jimmy Stephens was breathing easily in sleep. Then the cow, satisfied with her scrutiny, bore away to the left and soon he heard the soft plopping of falling cow-dung. Christy smiled and dropped down into uneasy sleep.

It was two-fifty-five by the phosphorescent face of his wrist-watch when the patrol leader of one of the bell-tents roused him. "Christy! Christy!" he called agitatedly, shaking the Scoutmaster's shoulder. "Christy!" the boy said, "Richie Maloney is retching off his stomach all the time." Christy slipped on his shoes and scrambled into his overcoat. He felt in the pocket of his overcoat for his torch. Outside, the night was possessed of a surpassing brightness. The sky above the sea that was previously powder-blue had now become suffused with a delightful apple-green. He had scarcely time to appreciate its curiousness when the night-air tentatively laid its keen blade across his skin. He flashed his torch through the tent doorway, picked out the patrol leader and another boy holding the sick scout upright in a sitting position. He stepped carefully among the still forms and put his arm around the sick lad's shoulder. He flashed the light full into the pale face, and the boy's reaction to the light seemed so unusual that he immediately switched off the torch. "What is it, Richie?" he wheedled. Then, "Lift him up!" he whispered to the other two. "Perhaps he'd be better off out in the air." The boy made no effort to put his legs under him, so Christy carried him in his arms.

Out in the air the sick boy brightened momentarily; then his head lolled heavily. The Scoutmaster slipped off his overcoat and threw it across Richie Maloney's shoulders. He helped him to a sitting position on a little mound near the wall. "Richie! Richie!" he whispered again. Then to the other two, "Call Jimmy Stephens and ask him to get the drop of brandy out of my case." One of the boys raced towards the white tent.

Christy began to speak softly to the sick lad: once again came the weary effort to raise the heavy head. The other Scout was whimpering with cold; Christy told him to put on some clothes. The boy went away quickly into the bell-tent. When he was alone with the sick lad Christy slewed him around until the moon was shining into the wan face. Suddenly the Scoutmaster noticed that the boy's weak bulbous tongue was ballooning out through the opening of his mouth. Before the cold significance of this could reach Christy's consciousness, the boy had begun to snore stertorously. Christy cupped his mouth against the boy's ear and clearly crooned out the Act of Contrition. His maternal eyes kept holding the boy's profile as if seeking, by the power of animal fascination alone, to pin the soul to life. But Richie Maloney suddenly added two terrifying inches to his size, deflated all the air that was in him in the ultimate throe, squeaked like a wet palm on a banister-rail, and died.

Christy held the boy for an unmoving minute after he knew that he was truly dead. The moon froze the pair to a piece of statuary, the sight of which chilled the two returning Scouts. "What is it, Christy?" Jimmy Stephens began anxiously, crouching down to the moonlit pair. The other boy was just beyond Jimmy's shoulder. Christy let the body sag a little. "He's dead!" he said. "Sweet God above!" said Jimmy, "How could he be dead? Why do you say that? He might only have fainted!" Jimmy put his hand against the inert head—it was now the head of a broken doll. In the background the patrol leader began to blubber. It was a chittering type of blubber. Jimmy Stephens began to cross himself over and over again. "But what'll we do, Christy? How'll we face home with him? Didn't his mother warn you to watch him carefully? We watched him, Christy, didn't we? The two of us watched him, Christy, didn't we?"

The morning was thrusting its great green fist into the sky. The inshore wavelets kept repeating "Lipss—lipss—lipss." A cock crowed from the fowl-runs behind the Castle.

Christy spoke to the patrol leader. "Val," he said, "get Tom Donnell's bike and ride for the priest. Ask the priest where the doctor lives and bring him too. Not that it's any use now, but . . . Hurry, Val, like a good boy."

Afterwards the affair became nightmarish. Christy carried the body into his own tent and covered it with a sheet. Jimmy Stephens and he took their clothes out into the dew-wet grass and dressed themselves. By now it was clear that the tragedy had communicated itself to the other Scouts. Heads appeared in the doorways of the bell-tents; a chorus of whispering broke out. It was difficult to know how the news of death had spread. Perhaps the subconscious is always sharpening its ear to hear it, senses are sharpened to apprehend it, a further dole of smell is kept in reserve to sniff new-made clay even through sleep, an extra access of sight is held in reserve to visualize (even through two canvas walls) a taut blue face and the final grimace of stripped teeth.

The Scouts were up and dressed and about without reprimand. They huddled in little frightened schools well away from the tent where the dead boy lay. A light twinkled in one of the windows of the Castle. The inquisitive cow munched nearer and nearer to the tent of death. No one raised a hand to frighten her away. The animal put a truculent head against the canvas and snuffed loudly. Christy took a step or two in her direction and stamped suddenly on the grass. The cow heaved out with astonishing agility. A figure with a lighted candle in its hand came to a window of the Castle. Then the lights of the priest's car were shining through the bars of the gateway. The gate clanged open and the tyres roared on the gravel.

Morning was upon them almost before they realized it. The owner of the Castle came down with his wife and led away the boys for a phantom meal. When later they emerged into the strengthening sunlight the old woman of the gateway was walking around in the dew-wet grass. She was tying and untying her fingers and calling out the Holy Name. People began to knot outside the white-barred gate. Two young women strolled east along the road. Each was swinging a blue bathing costume. When they learned the news from the people at the gateway the pair were pricked of their splendour and became ordinary frightened people. The boys looked up at the sun mounting behind the sandhills. The holiday was over. They set about taking down the bell-tents and piling their belongings. The little white bivouac was left standing, and the disconsolate lads sat dismally on their gear. The sea had a great sleekness to it. The thin mist of morning was vanishing; the long revolving lip of tide was increasing in whiteness. The boys looked wistfully at the sea, at the faint mountain-camps of the south, at the creamy flanks of the sandhills, at the long, attenuating scimitar of sand. Then they looked at the tent of death.

The Gap of Life

As the clock beneath the steeple in midsquare rustily banged four o'clock an old man emerged from a cottage set on a hillock on the edge of the town. It was a midsummer morning with the pale blue sky pricked with waning stars.

Wearing a long black overcoat over his pyjamas the old fellow shuffled forward on misshapen carpet slippers. He glanced along the cobbled ramp that rose from beside his doorway and vanished in a pathway that ran between the cottage gable and the high wall of a demesne. He moved to the kerbside and stepping down on to the narrow roadway glanced cautiously up and down.

The final humming of the clock strokes below had thinned out into silence.

Standing in mid-road and shading his eyes with his bladed hand so as to shut out the light of a nearby street lamp, the old man looked downhill for an appreciable space of time. At last he lowered his hand, shook his head and made as if to return to the doorway of the cottage.

The lock-lock of a bicycle straining as it moved uphill towards him caused the old man to hurry indoors.

The cyclist, a young man of twenty or so, was whistling softly. Just before he reached the cottage he dismounted and walked along the roadway wheeling his bicycle as he came. Noticing that the door of the cottage was not fully closed he slowed his pace somewhat and kept his eyes on the door. Gradually his footsteps idled to a halt. Resting his elbow on the saddle of the bicycle he continued to watch the door.

"Hey!" he called out at last. "You in there — are you okay?"

There was no reply.

The young man backed the bicycle until he was abreast of the doorway.

"You in there," he said, raising his voice, "are you okay?"

There was a long pause. At last, speaking from the darkness just inside the door the old man said in an even tone: "Yes, I'm all right."

The young man remained as he was for a few moments. "Is there anything the matter with you?" he asked, and then added rather lamely, "If it's the time you want it's just four o'clock in the morning."

There was no reply.

The young man muttered to himself and made as if to wheel his bicycle onwards. Then he stopped, propped the bicycle against the old stone kerb and stepping onto the raised pathway in front of the cottage walked cautiously back until he was again almost abreast of the doorway. He peered in.

"You still there?" he asked.

"Yes, I'm here," the old voice said.

"Are you sick? Or are you one of those fellows who can't sleep?"

"I'm not ill," the voice said. "And as a rule I'm a sound sleeper."

The young man hesitated, then said gruffly, "If that's the way you want it, that's the way you'll get it." He moved towards his machine but again turned on seeing the old man emerge and shuffle down onto the roadway.

Again the old fellow shaded his eyes with his hand and began to look downhill.

The young man examined the old man from his squashed slippers through his frayed pyjama ends, through his old-fashioned black velour-trimmed overcoat to his hollowed neck and grey hair. "Expecting some-one?" he asked suddenly.

"No! I don't think anyone will come. I don't think they'll even send a message."

"Who won't come? Eh? Who won't send a message?"

"*She* won't come . . . And those in charge — *they* won't send a message."

"Those in charge of what?"

"Those in charge of her."

"Her?"

"Yes, her!"

"I see," the young man said, in a puzzled tone of voice. The old fellow turned and said solemnly. "And then again she may even be going!"

"Going where?"

"Ah!" the old fellow said with a sad satisfaction. "That's the most difficult question in the world to answer."

"Coming or going you're likely to miss her now," the young man said. Then with a smile, "Ever hear what the chap said about the bus or the woman?"

"No!"

" 'If you miss a bus or a woman,' this chap said, 'don't worry your head for there's always another one coming'."

The young man shouted with laughter at his own joke.

"I won't have that talk!" the old man said sternly. "Be on your way whoever you are!"

"Whoever I am, is it? Easy now, old fellow. Simon is my name. Simple Simon was my nickname at school but whoever'ld buy me as a fool would want his money returned. I'm a fitter sent here to do a repair job on your creamery. Now, tell me your trouble."

"I've no trouble!"

"Then why are you out of your bed at this hour of a summer morning?" In a kindly tone. "Out with it!"

The old man paused. His face crafty, "I'd tell you only . . ." he began.

"Only what?"

"There are generations between us."

"What if there are? I'm human too. Look! I've two

hands, two legs and one head just like yourself. Various other organs as well. You and me have what old Brother Vexilla would call the common denominator of humanity."

"I didn't seek your company," the old man said inconsequently.

Simon turned wearily away. "Animal, vegetable or mineral?" he said as if to himself. Then turning, "It's your daughter, isn't it?"

"I've no children alive."

"It's your sister?"

"Not her either."

"The old woman who keeps house for you?" As the old man shook his head, "Who is it then?"

"It's my wife . . . she's ill."

"Where is she?"

"In St. Joseph's Hospital." He vaguely indicated the point in the landscape below where the hospital lay.

"Is she very ill?"

"She won't last this night," the old man said quietly. Then: "Come here, son! See that faint light in the hospital window? That's where she is. And I'm here . . . and not beside her at all. Now she and I who have been so long together are going our separate ways. And I can't help thinking . . ."

"What is it you can't help thinking?"

". . . that her hand should be in mine as she goes through the gap of life. I spoke to the Reverend Matron of the hospital . . ."

"What did *she* say?"

"She said 'Off home with you now, Timothy, and we'll do all that's needed.' I asked the doctor: he said the same. They didn't mean to give offence. But they didn't understand."

There was a short silence in which the old man lifted his face to the sky and added, "My wife was a great scholar."

"A scholar?" Simon echoed.

"A great woman to read stories."

"What kind of stories?"

"Best of all she liked legends."

"Legends?"

"Yes! legends from the east and from the west. She never grew tired of reading the story of Orpheus aloud for me."

"I never heard that story."

"It's a story from Ancient Greece. Orpheus called up his woman from the underworld. Her hand in his they walked upwards towards the light. And then, because he looked into her eyes too soon he lost her in the gap of life."

"Yes?"

" 'Eurydice!' he shouted just like that. But she was gone." The old man's voice trembled as he added: "I'm a kind of Orpheus now calling on Betty through the morning hours. 'Betty,' I say, 'Timothy is here! Give me your hand as you go out the gap of life . . .' "

"Sssh!" Simon said for the old fellow had been shouting. He added, "Will I stay here for a while and keep you company?"

"I'll be all right!"

"Is there anything I can do for you?"

"There's nothing *you* can do for me."

"Why not?"

"I don't wish to be rude. But *you* don't seem to be the kind of young man to do what I want done."

"What is it you want done?"

"You'ld only poke fun at me. It's different manners to-day. To you and those of your day women are playthings to be used and thrown aside. Not me!"

"You've roused my curiosity. Tell me what you want or I'll be angry with you."

There was a long pause. Timothy examined the face

of the young man. "You promise not to laugh at me?" he asked at last.

"I promise."

"The hospital gate is locked," Timothy said at last. "But if a lively fellow was to go around here by this cobbled laneway between my cottage and the desmesne wall and then travel along the railway line he'd find a chestnut tree with branches that dip over the hospital wall. That way he could get in."

"Go on!"

"He could steal through the kitchen-garden, pass the long rick of turf, come around by the gable of the building and then he'd maybe find the third window from the end . . ."

"That's where she is, is it?"

"Aye! The young man could even stand outside and peep in . . . And if he saw what I think he'd see, without himself being seen . . ."

"Yes?"

"He could open his hand like this; as if he was taking a woman's hand in his. And then he could say 'Eurydice!' "

"The woman inside — how can she hear him?"

"It doesn't matter whether she hears or not!" the old man said with intensity. As Simon shook his head, the old fellow added. "Don't you see? 'Twill be almost the same as if I was there myself."

Simon said wearily, "I think you should be said by the doctor and the nun."

"Good morning to you, son," the old man said. He turned his face towards the cottage door.

Simon took his bicycle and made as if to move away. He paused. "Eurydice," he said half to himself, "that's a fancy name." Addressing the old man. "Tell me—how could there be such closeness between you and her?"

"From being together always, we grew to have the one mind."

"The one mind?"

"Yes. If we were quiet in each other's company I'd say, 'You're thinking of the day we went together in the wagonette to Fenit Pier?'"

"Would you be right?"

"Yes! Another time if we were walking in silence along a country road, I'd say, 'It's your uncle Jim in Adelaide?'"

"Would you be right again?"

"I'd be always right. And then in the morning hours if she trembled and shouted 'Orpheus!' through her sleep I'd know she was afraid of this very morning. Then I'd take her hand in mine and she'd be comforted. Women can see beyond the grave far clearer than us men . . ." The old man fell silent for a while. Then in a humble tone he said, "I'm sorry for troubling you. You'll likely have a hard day's work in front of you. Good-bye, son."

He moved towards the door of the cottage.

"Wait!" Simon called out, placing his bicycle against the kerb.

"What is it?"

"The third window from the gable end? Eurydice?" As Timothy nodded, Simon said "I'll be back before you know it!"

Briskly he removed the bicycle clips from his trouser ends, buttoned his jacket and ran up the cobbled ramp.

The old man listened as the light sound of his sprinting footsteps grew fainter and fainter. He remained as he was for a few moments. He then shuffled to the point where the base of the cobbled ramp merged with the ground. Here the top of the little stone wall that edged the ramp was shaped like a low black polished stool with a railing of ribbon iron behind it. Facing the roadway, the old fellow seated himself on the dark stone, and shrivelled up his body until it seemed lost in the folds of his overcoat. He leaned his poll against the railing. His eyes closed.

The wheel of the heavens swung through all the intermediate stages of tint and hue between pale blue and young apple green. Stars and street light waned and the natural light of day began to come into its own. Sunk on his breast the old man's head gently fell and rose in sleep.

A motor-car stopped some distance away. There was the sound of muted mingled laughter — the deep laughter of a man and the rippling laughter of a young woman. There were low-keyed good-byes as the car drove off. The sound of the young woman's footsteps hurriedly approaching failed to awaken the old fellow.

The girl wore a dark cape above a flowing evening dress of pink chiffon. She moved with fluency. Seeing the sleeping figure she stopped in front of it, then, placing her hand on the old man's shoulder she shook him gently. "Sir!" she breathed. As Timothy's eyes opened, the girl said, "You'll catch your death sitting there!"

"Did he come back?" The old man's widening eyes showed fear.

"Did who come back?"

"The young man who owns the bicycle."

"There's no one here."

"He went on a message for me."

"What message?"

"He should be back long ago. What time is it?"

Just then the town clock struck five. Together the old man and the girl counted the strokes.

"Five!" Timothy said in dismay.

"He must return for his bicycle," the girl said. "Was it an important message?"

"Yes."

"Perhaps I can deliver it instead of him?"

"No! You can't deliver it at all." There was a pause in which Timothy first looked dully about him and then up into the girl's face. "I should know you," he said— "What's your name?"

"You know me, Timothy. I'm Hanna."

"Hanna? Hanna what?"

"Hanna Meehan. I'm a daughter of Tom Meehan the land steward. I live nearby — in the side-lodge of the demesne. I'm home on holidays from the University."

"I remember you now," Timothy said without conviction.

"You used to give me apples from your tree when I was small. 'Sweeteens' you called them. Remember?"

The old man's face opened in joyous clarity. "Oh!" he said. "Hanna Meehan— I have you now. You were so . . ." his hand crept out to indicate a child—"Dear God, are you grown so big?"

The girl laughed merrily. "I'm grown so big," she said, then added, "What's troubling you?"

"The madness of the old, that's all! Were you dancing, girl?"

"Yes!"

"Did you enjoy yourself?"

The girl's mouth made an indeterminate moue. "It was my first dress-dance," she said with something of disappointment to her tone. She caught the old man's hands in hers. "Your hands are cold. What are you waiting for?"

"My wife is ill in St. Joseph's. I couldn't sleep with thinking of her, so I sent a young man who was passing to see if she was gone or not . . ."

"I can phone from the lodge and ask the night nurse how she is. When I come back with word it will ease your mind."

The old man shook his head. "My message is different," he said.

The girl's sharp ears caught the sound of someone running in the laneway. "He's coming," she told the old man.

Simon came quickly round the gable-end of the cottage and onto the cobbled ramp. He stopped short on seeing the girl with the old man. Still keeping his eyes on her he came forward; he seemed somehow to resent finding his former intimacy with the old fellow broken.

"Well, son?" Timothy began.

"I found the tree," Simon said with obvious reluctance. "I crossed the wall. I came through the kitchen garden. I passed the rick of turf and turned the gable of the building. I stopped in the shadow outside the third window from the end."

"Yes?"

"The light in the ward was burning low. Her bed was just inside the window."

"Yes?"

"I stood there for a while. A nun dressed in white came along inside. She wore a crucifix and her rosary was rattling. She drew back the screen around the bed. A nurse came then and took the woman's pulse. She tightened her lips and nodded. The nun took a prayer book out of her skirt and began to read softly. The nurse answered the prayer."

"What was it she read?"

"The Litany . . ."

"I see. Go on."

"It went on and on. I thought 'twould never end. Then it was the *De Profundis* — *'Out of the depths I have cried to thee, O Lord.'* When that was finished another patient called. The two women put back the screen and went away. I watched your wife. She was breathing hard. 'Twas plain to see that she was stumbling through the gap of life."

"What then?" the old man asked softly.

Simon walked a little distance apart. The old fellow glanced at Hanna and then said in a firm tone. "Answer me! A woman always understands."

Simon, his face averted, kept looking into the distance.

At last he spoke. "I raised the window slowly. I stretched in my hand and caught her by the hand. Her hand was sweating and yet 'twas icy cold. Then in a loud whisper, 'Eurydice!' I said."

"Go on!"

"Her breathing stopped. 'Eurydice!' I said again. Then her hand tightened upon mine!"

"Tell out God's naked truth!" The old man's voice had exploded into a cracked shout. "That you may be crucified if you tell a lie!"

"God's naked sacred truth!" The young man had spun round and his voice came riding over the old man's outburst. "I tell you that her hand tightened on mine." There was a pause. Then he added quietly, "She gathered herself together then. She quivered a little . . ."

"Yes?"

"Then slowly she let go the breath. I waited for another breath. It never came. Her hand fell loosely by the counterpane. I drew back my hand. I lowered the window without sound and again I stood in the shadow."

"What else?" from Timothy.

"The nun came back. She took the woman's pulse. She looked at the nurse and shook her head. Then she drew the sheet up over the woman's face."

Timothy moved slowly to one side and looked downhill. "You played your part," he said slowly. He looked up at the morning sky. As if speaking to himself, he said: "I suppose I should say 'Lord have mercy on her.' But there are others who have said that." He turned to face the young man and the young woman. "Ye can be going now. Thanks to the pair of ye indeed."

"Can I make tea for you?" Hanna asked.

"Not if you don't want it yourself."

"I don't need it, thank you."

The old man nodded his head as if in thanks. Unexpectedly he raised his voice and began to sing quaveringly.

Thou hast gone from me, Eurydice,
Now my life is dark with fear . . .

As his voice broke off, Hanna moved to mid-road and looked up at the eastern sky. "One last star left," she said; then: "I have never been out at this hour of the morning before. So many wonderful things must happen while we're all asleep."

"She had the loveliest and the queerest sayings," the old man said.

"What kind of sayings?" Simon broke in.

"Sayings that had to do with men and women, with life and death and love. Things I could hardly tell a soul."

"And yet you say a woman always understands," Hanna said softly.

"That's true," Timothy conceded. After thinking for a while he added, "She used to say that a man wants but a woman wants to be wanted. And she used to say too . . ."

"Yes?" from Simon.

"About the things that call love into being — there's a big word for them — she used to say that the greatest stimulator of all was death."

"Why should she say a thing like that?" Simon asked.

"I couldn't be sure. I think it had something to do with it being the nature of woman to replace that which is lost. Will I tell ye where I first met her?"

"Yes!" both said softly together.

"I first met her in a wake-room. An old man was dead. Betty was going around the room carrying a silver tray of wine. I'll never forget her young face above that silver tray of wine." The old man turned and said vehemently: "I could have stretched out my hand and placed it on the corpse's face . . . and yet there was Betty, her face above the silver tray of wine and her two eyes whispering 'Replace! Replace that which has been lost!'

"What else would she say?" Hanna asked.

The old man gave a short whinny of laghter. "She said a woman was most truly a woman when, alone, she stopped to watch her reflection in a mirror. And at that she'd laugh at me and tell me to watch people."

"What do you mean — watch people?" Simon asked.

" 'If you watch every move they make you'll maybe understand!' — those were her words," the old man said.

"Understand what?" Simon asked.

"All about people, of course. What way their minds work. She'd tell me especially to watch how they moved. 'A man,' she'd say, 'as he walks, with every step he strikes the world a blow. But a woman, as she walks, she strokes the air just like you'ld stroke a cat. These small things,' she'd tell me, 'are everything.' "

"Everything?" softly from Hanna.

Timothy went on as if speaking from reverie. "She was a full woman to me!" he said, in proud and measured tones. "And in her own lovely cautious way she taught me how to be a full man to her. And so for me now, it seems that there are treasures everywhere, treasures in the time that that's gone and in the time that's as yet unrolled. Because of her I'm richer than Croesus in my memories."

"What you mean—these things are everything?" Simon insisted.

"And so they are," the old fellow said. "Aren't they among God's most precious gifts to man?" He looked directly at Simon. "Son," he said, "the clock of time is ticking on. Now maybe it's your turn to sit in the wake-room of the world and see a woman's face above a silver tray of wine." Turning to the girl, "And you, Hanna Meehan, pay heed to me! A man driving in a motor-car, every girl he meets on the road looks through the windscreen straight and true. And her eyes always find his! And with her eyes the girl asks one question and one question only."

"What question?" Simon asked impatiently.

"Don't tell him!" the girl broke in.

"What question does the girl ask?" Simon insisted.

"Her question is a straight and natural one — 'Is this the man who since the beginning of time was meant to fertilize my body?' All the words in the world lead to that question."

Simon roared with laughter. As the girl turned and looked at him with hatred in her eyes the young man broke off shamefacedly.

Timothy shuffled closer to Simon.

"Son!" he said, not without sadness, "You haven't even learned the ABC of life." Turning away and speaking as it were to himself he went on, "Lord have mercy on the dead, is it? No by God, but Lord have mercy on the living . . . on those with souls of smoke and bodies made of cork and minds like little Punch and Judy shows." Sensing that Simon was still smiling the old man rounded upon him. "Don't dare smile at me, my son!" he said in a loud voice. "I tell you that the many live out their lives frightened by cardboard giants towering above them in the dark. Heed me, the pair of you," he went speaking now in a tone of pleading. "Heed me, although I'm a cracked old man snared by a legend from the Grecian day and by the green morning walking up the sky . . ."

He looked about him in a puzzled manner as if there was something else he had forgotten to say. Then he shuffled forward and entered the cottage, quietly closing the door behind him.

Hanna moved a few steps and leaned her back against the low wall beside the stone stool on which the old man had fallen asleep. She pushed her head well back so that her hair rested against the narrow iron rail. Her long white throat was seen. Simon moved a few faltering steps that indicated that he hardly knew whether to go or stay.

"Him!" he said at last. The girl made no reply.

"Him! Would he be a wise man or a fool?" he tried again.

After a pause. "He's wise," Hanna said.

Simon pondered this for a few moments. "I'll admit this," he said, "he made a queer class of mood just now."

"Did he?"

"Aye! he did. But . . . I feel it going away from me now like a tide moving back into the sea." He laughed oddly. "And I'm not certain that I want that mood to go." He looked at the girl, then ventured to say, "Did you meet anyone special at the dance?"

After a pause, "No!"

"Oh!" Simon watched the girl for a few seconds and then said, "This mood that I was talking about — can it be captured and brought back again?"

"Moods come and go," the young woman said.

" 'Souls of smoke, bodies of cork, and minds . . . minds like what?' "

"Like Punch and Judy shows."

"Punch was the man—eh?"

"Punch was the man."

"He said that all words lead to it — what did he mean by that?"

"I don't know — unless you could guess, yourself."

After a pause, "Salmon!" the young man blurted in a loud voice. "There's a word that just came into my head. Salmon! How does the word salmon lead to what he was talking about?"

Hanna did not reply.

"You hear me, woman?"

"I hear you. That word might remind you of . . ."

"Of what?"

"Of a hen salmon fighting her way upstream against a torrent . . ."

"Aye! Fighting her way upstream to meet her destiny." Then: with an added sense of discovery, "Or beating her head against the gravel of the redd as she prepares to spawn."

There was a short silence. Then with a suppressed cry of triumph Simon said, "By God, I'm close to something that has dodged me all these years." He turned and looked for an appreciable space at the girl. Shyly he asked, "If I sat there beside you would you tell me the story?"

"What story?"

"You know well what story!"

"I do."

"Then why did you pretend not to know?"

"Protocol."

"What the hell is protocol?"

"The right way and the wrong." Her eyes fell. Not without wryness she added, "Protocol says that the man must ask. And that the woman must answer as if she didn't quite understand . . ."

"And then?"

"And then she must lead him on and on until at last she's completely sure."

"Hey!" Simon shouted as if in discovery. "I'll ask you so! Tell me the story of Orpheus and Eurydice." He moved swiftly towards the ramp and squatted at her feet. He looked up into the girl's face.

The girl began with a demure certainty. "Orpheus, son of a god, had the gift of music and of song. Wild beasts would turn and listen as he played upon his lute. The birds of the forest would fall silent at the first note he played at the break of day. He took Eurydice as his wife: she died and went down to Hades in the dark. He pleaded for her life and at last was told: 'You may go down into the underworld and find your wife. But do not look upon her face until you reach the mortal world above.' And so . . ."

"And so?"

"He took with him a ball of yarn and unrolled it as

he went down among the caves. At last in the darkness he reached her shade. 'Eurydice!' he cried and handed her the thread. 'Orpheus!' she said. Following the thread the man and the woman walked towards the light. Step after step upwards towards the light . . ."

The girl stood erect. Her face was averted. The young man rose and waited for her to resume.

"Just as they had reached the gap of life . . ." The girl's voice had broken off suddenly.

Gently and slowly Simon took her by the shoulder points and turned her round so that the first light of the morning sun burnished her features. "You're crying, woman," he said softly.

Angrily the girl tore herself free. As she raced up the ramp and hurried along the pathway between the desmesne wall and the cottage gable her voice reached him in tatters of anger and disappointment. "The fool!" she cried. "He broke the gods' taboo!"

Simon stood for an uncomprehending moment or two. Then he heard the voice of the old man singing faintly from the cottage.

> *Thou has gone from me, Eurydice*
> *Now my life is dark with fear.*
> *Grief and woe fill my soul*
> *Never more thy voice to hear*
> *Never more thy voice to hear . . .*

Simon turned from the closed door and glanced at the cobbled pathway along which the girl had fled. After a time he moved to mid-road and looked down towards the hospital building now illumined by the rays of the risen sun. Wearily he moved to the steps at the base of the ramp, placed each of his shoes in turn on the end of the low wall and replaced his bicycle clips.

He then wheeled his bicycle onto the road. Placing his footsole on the near pedal he hopped briskly onto the saddle. Softly he resumed his whistling as he rode away.

A Story That Spins

A man I knew only by sight joined me as I paced the
corridor of an angling hotel in the off-season. Falling into
step beside me, he interrupted my rehearsing a speech I
was due to make later that evening at a formal dinner in
the hotel.

"A middle-aged Civic Guard in my place," the man
began, his eyes reduced to bright points behind his
glasses, "told me the following story:

"The first station I was sent to was in a wild place in
the West of Ireland. The second or third evening I was
there, the Sergeant brought in the body of a baby which
had been found buried in a bog. The body was blue. The
Sergeant wrapped it in a newspaper and placed it on two
chairs in a little room off the day-room. I was orderly
that night: I slept in the dayroom bed. In the early hours
of the morning I heard a footstep on the gravel. Wearing
only my shirt and pants, I stole out by the back doorway
and came round by the corner of the building. A young
woman with a shawl on her shoulders had had her face
pressed against the window of the room in which the
baby's body lay. I said: "What are you doing there?" She
said: "I'm looking at my baby." I said nothing for a while.
Then I said: "You'd better be going!" The girl went
away."

"Why do you tell me this?" I asked the man.

"It might be of use to you."

"Use?"

"A Frenchman went around giving money for story
ideas like that. It's yours buckshee," he laughed.

"Thanks!" I said dryly. The man walked off.

With a sign to my wife, who, frozen after the car-
journey, was snuggled close to a big turf-fire, I resumed
my pacing of the corridor. The guests were arriving in
ones and twos. I halted at a window and, for a time
watched the moonlight remotely reflected on the surface

of the nearby lake. The last light of afternoon still dawdled behind the mountains.

—*Eire,* I began afresh, *Caitlín Ní Houlíhan, Pleasant Branch, Island of Saints and Scholars, Dark Rosaleen— for centuries these have been Ireland's unusual appellations in the mouths of her poets . . .*

The body is blue, I thought. It is wrapped in a newspaper. The mother—there is no sorrow in her standing there, only a black glory. Having risked discovery because of mother-love, will she return home, saying: "I dared! I am cleansed!" Saying also: "My all-love has churched me: now I can make a wholesome marriage and cast darkness into a corner of my father's barn."

Is this, then, the vision concealed in the tale? This, the dark flash? The woman, little more than a girl—is she mother, wife, sister, daughter and sweetheart of everyman? But—what does she stand to gain by this daring? Little? What does she stand to lose? All things? Is she not also woman all-trusting, despite recurrent hypocrisy and betrayal? If she is the flaw, she is also the mended flaw. If in human nature there is any faith, it is herein present.

—*Eire, our country, through the long centuries of slavery, when a lesser people would have tired of holding fast to the abstract idea of freedom, we Irish preserved intact the shining ideal.*

"Hallo, Ralph!" I said. Black suit, artist's cravat, red fed face, few would have believed that Ralph, now wholly citified in appearance, came from my own cowdung village.

"Hallo, Bomber! I see you're down to speak."

"God help Mother Eire!" I said. "You taking the pictures?"

"Aye! Any news from home?"

"No! Walk with me."

"Well, you see . . ."

"Walk, you bladder of lard!"

As we paced the corridor, I said: "A man came up to me a few minutes ago. He told me a story he had heard from a middle-aged Civic Guard." I went on to tell the tale.

For a time Ralph said nothing. I noticed that his yellow face had burned dark olive. "By God!" he said at last. Then, jerkily, "Why tell this story to me?"

"In every story like that, tnere is a button. If I can find it and press it, the story will open like a locket."

For a while we paced in silence. Then: "Maybe she was in the jigs after the infant had been dumped," Ralph said slowly. "When she had learned vaguely that the body had been found, the hell of not knowing for certain how things were was worse than the purgatory she had already gone through. She *had* to look in that window whether she liked it or not."

"She was forced, by her own emotions, to look in?"

"Women are at the mercy of those things," Ralph went on quickly. "Remember the heifer and calf in the O'Flaherty story?" "No vision, then?" I asked. "Vision, my eye! A month later she nearly went crazy at the thought of the risk she had run." "I never thought of that." "You can be certain that she had calculated to a hairsbreadth the result of her apparent gamble." "Calculation doesn't tally with the heifer and calf," I said; "or with your certainty of near-craziness afterwards." "How can you tell with these bloody women anyhow?" Ralph answered. "All I know is that she had sized up the young Guard to a T: if it was another woman had found her at the window she'd never have confessed. You see, she was balanced on the see-saw of sex." "The Yanks have debased the word," I laughed and then added: "But she could very well have met the Sergeant. The young Guard was in the station for a few days only. I'm not convinced that there wasn't an element of a gambling bravery in her action." "Gamble nothing!" Ralph said. "Bravery less than nothing! She knew that if she met anyone it would be a man." "It may have seemed a certainty to us viewing it afterwards," I said, "but it was hardly a certainty to her pondering it before." Ralph shook his head and glared in front of him.

Suddenly he stopped and looked me in the face. "I got a bit of a fright that way myself once."

"I never knew that."

"You were reared odd," he said. "Your ould fellow was wearing a kilt and recruiting for the Celtic Brethren," Ralph laughed harshly. "I sweated blood," he added, and began walking away.

I walked after him. "A little Coneffe lady from the Potteries . . . I nearly went out of my mind," Ralph muttered.

"One of those girls died young."

"Clean out of my mind."

"The child?"

"What child?" Ralph blazed.

"The child in the story?"

"Oh! Natural causes. You can be sure of it."

"No vision?"

"No vision," he said. "It's a story that goes nowhere. Except maybe it goes round in a circle. That's it," he said eagerly. "It's a story that spins." His attention tailed off. I found him looking towards the hallway, where a slim young woman was doffing her fur coat. "Your profile isn't bad," he said, with a sly glance at me. "I'll wangle a picture of you into the newspapers. Good luck, Bomber."

"Good luck, Ralph!"

—*Such a deathless tale as that which tells of the affection Diarmuid of the Love-spot bore for Gráinne, or the legend which tells of the loyalty of the Sons of Usnach who stood shoulder to shoulder to protect Déirdre of the Sorrows— these are stories that shall never perish from the memory of our people.*

—The body is blue. The Guard is dressed only in his shirt and pants. He has the carriage of a hurler. An air of innocence accompanies him. Very likely his father is a tradesman, a carpenter who has struggled to see his son rise in the world. The old man dreams his son a Sergeant, an Inspector or even a Superintendent. The young man stands in the moonlight, his hair crisp about his ears. Charity is implicit in the drooping of his mouth-corners. Acting as God would have acted—how can this young man ever grow old and gross?

—*When at Fontenoy the French were forced to yield step after bloody step, then it was that gallant Lord Clare, standing up in his stirrups, cried out: "Irishmen! Recall the breached walls of your beloved Limerick! Recall the Treaty broken ere the ink wherewith 'twas writ was dry."*

"Hello, Mary!" I said. "Hello, Ted!" "You look wonderful, Mary." "You never lost it, you thief!" After a glance of concern at the bar-room door, Mary said: "Walk with me, Ted. I'm famished waiting." "Is he still on it?" "Hell-hard! Walk with me, Ted. Cover up." "I meant to walk with you anyway, Mary." "Did you?" "Yes. But I wasn't altogether altruistic." "I thought as much." "I want to ask you something." "Too late to ask me anything." "Not that, Mary." "You're going to grill me," she smiled. "It's because you're a woman," I said. "Discovery!" she said. "You look wonderful, Mary. I mean it." "Thanks!" she said quietly.

"A chap walked up to me a few minutes ago," I said, "and told me a story." I told Mary the tale.

"What do you want to find out?" she asked.

"I don't know."

"Still looking for the vision?"

"Well, that's not so strange. In the old churches . . ."

"In the old churches," she began to chant, "there was a room high in a wall above the sanctuary. Here lepers crouched on Sundays squinting down at the altar, which was ablaze with flowers and lights. If only I can find the lazar-squint which hangs above this story . . ."

"I'm a prize simpleton," I said ruefully.

"I often meant to ask you, Ted. What do you want this vision for?"

"To see—as God sees."

"Why wish to see as God sees?"

"To widen the circle of human experience. To . . ."

"Yes?"

"To spirit-spill into my neighbour."

"As precious as ever, Ted."

"In this story, the Guard forgives . . ."

Urgently: "He releases the girl under the Cat-and-Mouse Act."

"Why?"

"He was not above emotional blackmail."

"A sin against charity, Mary."

"Where's the charity? Where's the truth? This young Guard takes an oath to see justice done. He perjures himself on one of his earliest nights of duty."

"Mm-m."

"Looking at the girl's face, the Guard thinks: 'I've a grip on you, my lady!' " "A shabby vision, Mary." "Shabby people are in the majority." "Will the Guard press home his blackmail?" "Not necessarily, but it gives him satisfaction to have the devil's guinea in his purse." "I was looking for something better, Mary." "A vision?" she spat, "maybe a vision of hell." "With you it's conjecture, as it is with me." "With me it's knowledge," Mary said. Then, eyes on fire she faced me. "Remember the night I first wore the lace dance-frock? At Durren Tennis Dance. I fought with you that night, Ted. I went out with . . ." She broke off and added bitterly: "With me it's not guesswork. One can tell for certain that frog-spawn always grow into frogs."

We had come to a halt in front of a glass-case in which large trout were on exhibition. "It's no use," she grimaced. "Your story won't march. It will go round and round. Twist it, twirl it. When the wheel stops you'll find the pair static in the moonlight."

"I'll keep trying."

"Do that!" she said. "But remember that if your lovely Guard grows old and rises in rank some woman shall live in terror of such occasions as public dinners."

I said nothing. "Still wall-boxing, Ted?" she said. "Shadow-boxing, Mary." "It's all the same—shadow or wall." The bar-room door opened. A brawl of voices emerged. With a sigh: "Good luck, Ted!" "Good luck, Mary!" Walking as delicately as a thoroughbred filly, Mary walked away.

—When the dark raven on the sails of the marauding Danes was seen from our shores, then was set an end to one facet of the golden way of life our forefathers had evolved. When on a morning of racing rain at Kinsale the chiefs were defeated, the shining shards of our culture were ground to dust beneath the invaders' heel. When . . .

The body is blue. Ill-luck aside, would this child have grown up to beauty and lissomeness? In a quiet country-side, would he have been graceful in the inverted beauty of his shadowed origin?

Is it not wholesome to recall the mythical heroes of our Race? Young Setanta on the road to Emhain Macha: his spear, his hurley, his hurling ball of shining gold. A blow and the ball sings into the blue. A flash and the stripling's spear divides the sky; a happy-go-lucky flight of ash into air—look! the hurley is looping and leaping in the morning light.

A girl of seven or so went hopping by. "Hallo!" she said, stopping to look up at me. "Hallo, 'Tricia! How's your knee?" Primly showing the white mark on the knee-cap: "It's better, thank you." "You've grown since last spring," I said. "Yes; I'm a big girl now." "How's Donkey-Nicholas?" I asked. "He's fine, thank you." I made to pace away, but did not wish to appear rude to the child. "Will you come again when the season opens?" the dark-haired dark-eyed girl asked. Solemn in navy-blue jersey and tartan skirt, she continued to gaze up at me.

"Yes, if my work is finished." "What work do you

do?" "I write stories and things." "Like 'Puddlefoot'?"
I laughed. "Are you writing a story now?" "In my head
only." "What's the story about?" "It's about . . . Sit here,
'Tricia."

Together we sat on a carved box by the side of the
corridor.

"It's about a little girl." "What's her name?" "Her
name is Oona: she got a blue-eyed dolly for her birthday."
"Could it say 'Mama'?" "Yes . . . but she lost her dolly."
"How did she lose it?" "She was playing on the moun-
tainside. She forgot to bring the dolly home." "Oh!"

"I must tell you how it was," I went on. "That night
Oona had a dream. She dreamt that Guard Culleton had
found her dolly and had brought it to the station. The
guard put the broken dolly on a chair. The little girl sat
up in bed long after midnight. 'My dolly is in the Garda
Station,' she said. 'I saw her in my dream. She is broken.
I must go to my dolly at once.' Ooona did not tell her
daddy or her mammy where she was going. She stole
downstairs and went softly down the village street. The
moon was shining.

"Oona peeps in the window of the barracks." I made
the movement of peeping.

"Is the dolly there?" the girl at my side asks, her eyes
fixed firmly on my face. "The dolly is there but it is
broken." "Can it say 'Mama' now?" "No, it is badly
broken." As Oona begins to cry, I add quickly, "Guard
Culleton comes round the corner of the building—he
has heard the girl sobbing outside. 'What are you doing
here, Oona?' he asks. 'I'm looking at my dolly,' the girl
says. 'You can't get your dolly now — you must wait
till morning.' 'I do not want her now,' Ooona says; 'I
just came to see her.' 'Please go home, Oona,' Guard
Culleton says. 'May I look at her again?' Oona asks.
'Better hurry up about it: the Sergeant might hear us
talking.' So Oona presses her face against the glass and
looks in once more. Then she returns home."

After a pause, 'Tricia said: "Feeny Rackert threw my dolly down the old lime-kiln. I peeped over. The dolly was away down among the bushes."

"What did you do?"

"I sat by the bushes and cried."

"That's what Oona did."

"I know," the child said, her eyes large and solemn. "Then I heard Mr. Devere shouting from his front lawn. He had his hands to his mouth. Like this! So I crept between the bars of the gate and stole away."

"Why did you cry?"

"Because I was lonely. The dolly's name was Josephine. What was the name of Oona's dolly?"

"She hadn't got a name—it's just a story."

"Oh!"

"Did you tell your Daddy, 'Tricia?"

"No! Daddy said I wasn't to play near the limekiln."

"So you cried?"

"Yes, I cried and cried. I sat down by the black bushes."

For a while 'Tricia and I were silent and contemplative. I spied a single tear poised on the lower lashes of one of her eyes.

At the corridor's end a door swished open. I caught a glimpse of a bright red toy horse. With a word of farewell the girl beside me bounced up and made off.

—*When at the very end of anguish it seemed as if Ireland were a corpse on the dissecting table: when all hope was utterly lost, then was heard at Eastertide the voice of a poetic band proclaiming a nation's resurrection.*

—The body is blue.

I came suddenly to my feet. I felt angry with the hotel which was now a buzz of greeting and conversation. Beside me a doorway gave to a lawn. I went out into the night. The far angle of the lake was smudged with the reflection of the upcoming moon. The night was cold. Cudgel, I counselled myself, then: Court! Threshing in my mind, clue-seeking, I thought of many things: of Ormuzd, the chief god of the ancient Persians, of gangrene, ospreys, pawnbrokers, hugger-mugger and scalene triangles. But all the while the young man and the young woman remained in tableau directly in front of me. "Cush!" I said, as an old woman would say to venturesome hens. "Cush!" once more. Vainly! The couple continued to outblaze the moonlight.

At mouth-height behind me a cigarette glowed. The man who had told me the story had come on to the lawn. I again saw the points of shine behind his glasses. He inhaled deeply on his cigarette. With the exhalation: "Still puzzling?" "Ay!" I said. The man laughed: again the cigarette blazed. "Isn't there something more?" I asked; "some clue you've overlooked?" He shook his head. "A clear stage. Nothing missing that should be present; nothing present that should be missing." Then, looking directly at me: "What exactly is your trouble?"

"The story won't proceed. It *may* spin; but when the wheel stops, there they are, set fast in a pattern of indigo and silver." "Shatter them!" he said. "How?" "With a grenade," he said.

My eyes followed his outstretched cigarette hand. "The white building," he said: "the Guard and the girl — their gazes locked. The window . . . the grenade is in your hand. Pull the pin and toss it between them." The man left me abruptly.

I closed my eyes. When again I opened them the tableau was clearer than before. I felt the grenade urgent in my palm. I gritted my teeth, squeezed hard on the missile, brought clenched hands together, pulled the pin and with a quick swing dropped the grenade right between the man and the woman.

The explosion blew them to smithereens. After the flame-bang came the smoke and the smell. When again the moonlight was tolerably strong, I found that the young man and woman had disappeared. The walls and windows of the building were undamaged. The night grew quiet. I felt victorious.

I heard a faint padding from within the building. I heard a scrape of toenails and a "huh" of infantile exertion. Weak fingers gained purchase on the window frame. Then I saw the blue features of an infant framed in white woodwork. The face seemed as if a nylon stocking had been pulled right over it and a blue spotlight directed upon it from above. I was conscious of growing intensely curious.

"Hallo!" the blue lips said.

The greeting reached me as if there were no glass in the window frame. "There was a bench here," the infant went on. "I got on to it and pulled myself up." He looked about him in satisfaction. "You made short work of the pair," he said. I nodded. "A writer, eh?" Again I nodded. He glanced to the left: "She sinned," he said; he glanced to the right: "The other fellow sinned, too." His eyes fast on me: "You sinned most of all," he grinned. "I?" "Yes. Usurping the urbanity of God. Jostling Christ from off His Judgment Seat. Pride of the intellect and all that." Patiently: "Don't tell me that those are not sins." I said nothing. For a moment or two the infant lost his blue grin. Then precariously he tried placing his cyanosed fingers to his head. "Limbo skull unclosed," he complained good-humouredly. "I'll make a poor show on Judgment Day." Still grinning: "How many times in thought have you brought me and mine into blue life? How often have you buried us in bogs, our skulls un-knit, our heads lolling under newspapers?" Then: "Cudgel and court!" he mocked. From the point of his tongue he spat quickly upwards. On my cheek a fleck of spittle bubbled. I raised my hand to to remove it. "It won't scald you," he laughed; "it's as light as lime." He lowered himself from the window. I heard him stumping uncertainly in the room. I heard the newspapers rustle.

A gong rang. I spell-broke and went in. "What's wrong?" my wife asked. "An ache in my poll," I said; "it'll pass." I sat down to dinner. Mary winked at me from across the table. The girl 'Tricia showed herself for a moment in the doorway. When the meal was over, I made my speech. Ralph took the pictures, then gave me the vee-sign that all was well.

Driving home at daybreak, our car struck an ass-foal in a mountain pass. I left the vehicle to see what I could do. My wife's anguished face was pressed against the windshield as she watched the furry shape kick its last in the fan of the wan headlights. After I had laid the dead animal on the road-edge, we continued our journey in silence. Around us for miles the boulders had begun to be touched by the first grey of day.

Black Nets

As the tide brimmed slowly in, its mounting green fluid began to shorten the long-legged cliffs. Far out in the dazzling western world sky had mated with water until the horizon was imagined rather than seen. To the north and south small clouds, no larger than gun-puffs, decorated the heavens. Over the strand the gulls moved beautifully, the blades of their outstretched wings finding the grain of the timber sky.

The seaside resort nestled under the northern cliffs. Southwards the fawn strand flowed in a curve that was roughly three miles in length. The strand ended on the slobby estuary of a river beside which lay the fishing village—an excrescence of tarred sheds and thatched cabins. Beyond this huddle, on the other side of the river, loomed a large hill dotted with lime-washed cottages. Seaward from the estuary the southern horizon was formed mostly by the bell-tents of three mountain peaks. To-day these peaks were gauzed in sun-heat.

The sandhills between the seaside resort and the fishing village were divided equally into two zones of influence. Southward for a mile and a half went the golf links—the undulating emerald axminster links. Standing on one of the many domesticated dunes they contained, one saw the admirable switchback sweep of the fairways, the flawless cosy greens (each decorated with a brilliant red pennant), the tortured and defeated bent-grass, the collapsed and untenanted rabbit-holes (untenanted, for the rabbits had been efficiently gassed). The whole course seemed to be whispering the word "Civilization" over and over as if it were a prayer. For the greater part of its southward journey the links saw to it that they kept a stout dune between them and the uncivilized sea. But the thirteenth green, like a foolish

100

virgin, peeped out over the sandy cliff and recoiled
astounded at the barbarity of what it had seen. Instantly,
the links swung inwards and northwards towards home,
sauntering unadventurously through the smooth fields.

But southwards from the thirteenth hole the sandhills
were untamed bristling upheavals of scabby, mangy
ground that brightened with a thousand rabbit-scuts on
a sudden handclap. Here and there the dunes were
slashed into huge valleys of dazzling white sand—the
sand studded by the further brightnesses of shells and
stones and bones. This savagery of land raged and
roared southwards till it whimpered out in blown sand
beside the fishermen's cottages on the estuary.

A boat was hauling on the Long Strand a few hundred
yards to the south of the thirteenth hole. As the boat
moved out to sea it cut the flecked flanks of waves of
average strength, which lifted, then lipped tentatively,
finally spilling like tumbled churns of milk. The boat
itself was of an unusual make, rather resembling a
canoe in timber: like the canoe it had a high prow and
stern. It was called a "ganelow", which word, as likely
as not, was a corruption of "gondola". The three fishermen in the vessel were Pompey Connors and the two
Cournanes. A youngster of sixteen or so named Danny
Martin was standing on the strand "shoring", that is,
he was holding the head of the net-rope. The men were
fishing for the rearguard of the spring salmon or the
vanguard of the peal.

Pompey Connors was as black as the hob of hell; he
had a squat powerful body. His arms were the arms of
an ape. Under the visor of his dirty cap the two jet pupils
of his eyes were set in startling whites that might have
belonged to a Negro. The whites were terrifying in the
sooty stubble of his face. His eyes, the old people said,
had not been given him for his soul's salvation. His lips
made the letter *s* lying on its side: they had been
twisted either by a cerebral stroke or by an unusually

sardonic outlook on life. When his great mouth opened it was seen to contain a ruined temple, with the broken amber pillars of his teeth fallen haphazardly on the red sand of his gums.

The two Cournanes were cousins, a fact proclaimed less by their red colouring than by the similar bone construction of their faces. One, who was perhaps fifteen years older than the other, had begun to acquire the grizzle of the forties; the younger of the two was dressed in a suit of rags. Both cousins were barefooted. Pompey wore heavy old boots with uppers well slashed to let the sea water in and out.

After a morning of fruitless fishing Pompey and the younger Cournane left the boat and walked up the sand. Danny Martin turned southwards and went in the direction of the village. The older Cournane remained in the boat. He had shipped the unwieldy oars and was resting his weight across one of them. The younger Cournane mooched disconsolately about the sand; he picked up a belt of madra-ruadh seaweed and began to pull it apart in his spatulate fingers. Tiring of this, he looked out to sea. He called Pompey's attention to a large flock of gulls attacking something in the sea about four miles from the shore. After hooding his eyes and looking out to sea for a space, Pompey said it was a school of mullet or else a dead sea-pig. That ended the conversation between them.

Between the sandhills and the sea was a great rampart of rounded stones which raised itself in three distinctly marked tiers. Pompey threw himself down on the lowest tier, took out a shortened pipe and began to smoke. After a while the younger Cournane also threw himself on the stones, about thirty yards south of Pompey. Lying down he looked like a bundle of old clothes or the body of a drowned sailor cast up by the sea. As Pompey smoked, his eyes instinctively sought the resort under the dark northern cliffs. His gaze lingered thought-

fully on the white hotels with annexes that looked like
children's arks or playboxes painted lime green. He slipped
deeper and deeper into rumination.

Half an hour passed thus. Pompey's pipe grew cold in
his palm. His eyes had grown as soft as a cocker's. Then
young Cournane came up. "I might as well get the jar
for you," he ventured deferentially.

"Aye, you might as well," said Pompey, not without
surliness. He spat as he looked out at the barren sea, at
the boat slumped at the tide's lip, at the irritating figure
of the older Cournane crouched over the oar.

As young Cournane took the earthenware jar from
under the stern or "deck," his cousin lifted his face
and ran his tongue over the salted crevices of his lips.

Returning to Pompey the young man set the jar down
on the sand. Pompey's ruined yet powerful mouth was
opened in a grimace of twisted humour. Cournane
waited respectfully while Pompey built up an effect by
scrutinizing some coins in his palm. Then the dark face
twisted towards Cournane.

"Did you ever hear what the mountainy man said as
he looked at his sow?" asked Pompey.

"What was that?"

"He said, 'God direct me whether I'll ate you or
drink you'."

"Ha-ha-ha," went Cournane's raucous laughter. Then
"Ha-ha-ha" again. Pompey looked at the sycophant in
open disgust. Cournane's glee puttered and ceased.
Pompey rose and spat on the sand. He gripped the jar
by the ear and strode up the hill of rounded stones.
Though he did not make noise by displacing even a
single stone, the older Cournane lifted himself in the
boat and watched him until he disappeared through a
gap in the wall of the dunes.

A long time after he had gone a woman in a rose-red
ruched bathing costume walked down the strand towards
the boat. She was a young woman and her fair hair was

sculped in the air behind her. Every movement of her
body gave glory to God. Gradually the man in the boat
raised himself to watch her. A head appeared on the
bundle of rags on the stones. When the woman was perhaps a hundred yards from the boat, she turned abruptly
and walked away.

As he was returning from the resort with the jar of
porter, Pompey cut diagonally across the golf links. This
was a route he had never before taken, but to-day he
found the jar a load on his cramped fingers, and besides,
the heat of the sun was beginning to suck the sap of
strength out of his body. He began to tingle and smile
as he felt the elastic pile of the grass beneath his heavy
boots. He was experiencing the thrill of the unchallenged
trespasser. Whenever he put down his boot he churlishly
saw to it that he placed it on a shrivelled daisy or on a
tiny winsome heartsease. Once or twice he laughed
aloud. Suddenly he felt an urge to trumpet a challenge
into the green corridors of the links. He walked on to a
green, and then it seemed to him that he was a burglar
in a bedroom of a mansion. He lifted the flag-pin out of
the hole and speared it home. It fell with a clang into the
metal cup.

At first he was taken aback on finding a four-ball
approaching the thirteenth green. His tendency to halt
was a natural reaction, but he overcame it and walked
forward with hooded menacing eyes. The men were
approaching the green; the nearest man to Pompey was
a short stout man dressed in a fawn windbreaker and
black trousers. Pompey walked out into the rough and
drew level with this man as he was taking an iron from
the caddy. Pompey noted the sun-crimsoned fleshy face
with its protuberant eyes, the greying head and the
stumpy neck on the bottle-neck shoulders. Pompey was
momentarily puzzled by the whiteness of the man's
throat. Then the black pants the golfer was wearing led
him to the conclusion that the man was a priest. The

priest seemed to be labouring under a sense of grievance, for his lips were pouted and the preliminary swings of his club conveyed a sense of ill-temper. The caddy's face, too, was extra alert to anticipate displeasure: at the slightest glance by the priest in his direction he was quick to feign apprehension.

Pompey sauntered past the priest. His pace lagged down as he waited to watch the stroke. The priest gathered himself in a lump over the ball and began to address it. He broke his stance and looked at Pompey as if requesting him to cease walking. As the golfer resumed his position, Pompey halted; this seemed to disconcert the priest much more than the walking had done. Pompey rolled his tongue in his mouth and hissed softly through his nose. After the priest had played and failed to make the green he looked at Pompey as if blaming him for the mishap. Pompey's dark eyes coolly took the reprimanding glance, and as the priest moved up to the green he followed leisurely, all the while keeping at a discreet distance in the rough. The priest's next stroke brought him to within a yard of the pin. Pompey was now squatted on a small dune over the sea with the green directly beneath him; he had laid down the jar, and his eyes were firmly fixed on the golfers. Again the priest began his ungainly address, but he seemed to be irritated immoderately at finding himself thus gaped at by the fisherman. His brogues became uneasy and unsatisfactory; the movements of his head and body frankly expressed disgust. At long last came the ill-timed loose tap that muffed an easy putt. None of the others commented on this. As the priest bent and snatched up the ball, his eyes roamed to measure his companions' reactions. Then he looked up at Pompey on his perch. His face hardened, for he fancied that the fisherman was smiling at him.

As the golfers drove to the fourteenth, Pompey still retained his position and eagerly watched the balls rise gracefully in long parabolas and fall far down the fairway. All except the priest's, which swung determinedly in a powerful yet graceless curve into a bunker to the left. Again his eyes put the blame on Pompey.

There was a workmanlike rattle as the caddies slung the bags high on their shoulders. The sudden noise seemed to break the tension. Then Pompey's face hardened; he rose from his crouch, walked forward slowly but deliberately, and placed himself in the priest's road. At first the priest could scarcely credit the obvious fact that the fisherman was bent on obstructing him. Then, after the perceptible pause that followed on this incredulity, he steeled his face for a rebuke. But although Pompey was fully equipped to read the portents in the priest's face, he stubbornly stood his ground. His boots were rooted in the turf. He did not consider it his duty to raise his cap since the priest was not wearing his collar. When at last the fisherman spoke there was no trace of servility in the tone of his voice.

"You'd better do something for us, Father," he demanded.

The priest's brows came down abruptly. He was having trouble with his refractory mouth. "Do something for ye?" he asked.

"Aye! do something for us!" Pompey's voice was now coloured with a deep emotion.

The priest hesitated. Anger or tolerance? Curiosity and his training for the priesthood urged him to be tolerant. He was aware that his companions had halted and had become acute witnesses of the little duel. At last he raised his eyebrows in the most tolerant of unspoken queries.

For answer Pompey curtly nodded downwards and indicated the boat riding at the tide-lip. "Black nets!" he said.

The priest looked down. He saw the idle boat with the man asleep across the oar. He saw the ragman slumped on the round stones. He saw the youngster returning from the fishing village. Turning again to Pompey he looked him up and down. His gaze stole towards his fellow golfers.

"Oh!" he said, almost making the fatal error of laughing. Then, with remote amusement, "What do ye want *me* to do for ye?" His face had bloomed up in the full flower of tolerance.

Pompey's reply came with the accuracy and speed of a cobbler's hammer. "That'd be more your business than mine, Father," he said.

Under his summer crimson the priest's colour momentarily changed. He opened his mouth to speak, but thinking better of it, drew in a quick breath and clamped his teeth tightly together. Air came from his nostrils as he walked round Pompey and drew away to join his companions.

Pompey was left on the higher ground. His jar of porter lay behind him on the turf. His face had darkened to malevolence. His eyes had become objects that could inspire terror. Despite the great heat of the day he had begun to tremble. His rose tongue (a peacemaking woman) crept out to quieten the brawling masculinity of his lips. He stood there watching the players walk away into the grassy hollows. Far below him he saw the priest approach his ball, saw him select a niblick from his bag, saw him crouch, saw him strike, saw the ball lift over a small dune, saw it bound dead on the pin. As Pompey watched, his broken nails were digging into his palms.

The excellent stroke restored his buoyancy to the priest. It brought gaiety back to his carriage. It was as if the loose faggots of his nerves had been suddenly bound in a trim bundle. He was walking sprucely up to the green when, inexplicably, he halted dead in his stride. He turned and looked back at the dark figure on the dune. For a moment it seemed as if Pompey and

the priest were alone in all creation. Their thoughts
began tangling and twining across the intervening space
like seaweed swaying on the sea-bed.

Then, of a sudden, the priest turned seaward, raised
his hand, and scrawled curiously in the sky. The golfers
watched him intently, even embarrassedly.

As for Pompey, he began to laugh like hell. Grabbing
up his jar of porter he commenced to run awkwardly.
Out through the fawn gap in the dune wall he ran,
while the loose sand tried in vain to clog his passage.
He plunged down the slope of stones, making a great
racket as he moved. Seeing him, the boy returning from
the village began to quicken his pace, the sleeper in the
boat raised himself, and the bundle of rags on the stones
began its resurrection.

Pompey placed the jar on the sand and then laughed
richly out into the tide. He was shouting at the
Cournanes: "We'll try one more haul!" Then, as a
surprising after-thought, in a curious tone of voice ". . .
in the name of the Father, Son and Holy Ghost." The
Cournanes looked at him: their dullard lips were wide
apart.

Pompey leaped into the boat and paid out the net as
the two Cournanes rowed. Danny Martin held the net
rope on the strand. "Pull, blast ye, pull!" roared Pompey.
When he stood erect in the boat he seemed to dominate
the sea. The circle was quickly completed, and jumping
out into the shallow water, Pompey and the elder
Cournane began to close the haul while the younger
Cournane joined Martin. Slowly the necklace of
blackened corks moved in-shore. Even the incurious
Cournanes began to show signs of excitement. Their
eyes lost their natural stupidity and their mouths
widened in a strange sagacity. They took a pace or two
nearer the net and were soon up to their collops in the
tide.

It was then Pompey began to roar, and the noise his

mouth made was like the sound of a hound baying. He was pointing here and there along the dwindling semi-circle of half-submerged corks. Then, as on a signal, the great school of trapped salmon began to drive smoke out of the net.

A cormorant flew low across the sea. Its flight was determined and urgent. Over the horizon hung a great cloud and from behind it the sunlight streamed down in seven strong shafts.

The Corn Was Springing

The boy heard the young footsteps behind and beneath him. Then he heard the tittering like tearing paper. When the footsteps stopped he dared not turn round though he was aware that the eyes behind and beneath him were gimleting holes in his shoulder-blades. As he turned, a fistful of spalls was thrown in his face: a sharp stone caught him on the cheek bone. He blinked his eyes protectively. When he opened them again he had a memory of two dresses whisking beneath his little scaffold and vanishing through the chapel door. He heard the inner glass door swish open. Within the chapel the first footsteps of his attackers were excited and irreverent. The door was a long while closing, as it was controlled by an apparatus designed to prevent it slamming. Then he heard the footsteps within grow reverent and meek and innocent. The boy put the back of his hand to his cheek where the spall had nicked him; when he withdrew it there was a small sign of blood on the point of the knuckle. He resumed his carving on the hood moulding around the doorway. As he worked he hummed menacingly through his teeth:

> I'm sitting on the stile, Mary, where we sat side by side,
> On a bright May morning long ago when first you were my bride.
> The corn was springing fresh and green . . .

Through the song and the noise of the mallet his ears were most alert.

The convent, with the chapel to the right of it and the schools to the left, was wonderfully clear in the pure air of the May morning. The three buildings formed a quadrangle with an open side or mouth. This mouth was turned to the south: thus the sunlight of the young summer was trapped in the garden beds before the convent door. In the middle of the beds was a statue of Our Lady. Around the base of the statue was a bed of tulips, already alight with vivid blooms which leaped up from a carpet of forget-me-nots. The façade of the convent proper was scrawled over by the angry cords of Virginia creeper which in autumn whooshed the sober building into a red-gold blaze. The high convent peeped over the ivied wall into the village, the single street of which fell downhill to peter out in a mutter of thatched cottages at the base of the hill.

The planks on which the boy was seated were supported by two six-foot trestles. The youngster appeared to be about seventeen years of age. He was wearing a soiled white coat. A pair of goggles was pushed high up on his forehead. He had an open, even a merry face. Soon the anger ebbed in him and he began to forget that he was waiting for his assailants to emerge. He focused his attention on the mallet and chisel. This was the first time the foreman had entrusted him with important work of this nature and it behoved him to be careful. He continued to sing softly, but the malice had now vanished from his song; "The lark's loud song is in my ear and the corn is green again." The mallet wasn't a whit too heavy for his hand: it was accurate, obedient, and kind, going where he asked it to go. Funny to listen to the old stone-cutters talking of mallets. Holly was good, American hickory better, but neither the one nor the other could hold candlelight to the wood of the female crab-tree. The old fellows on the job were a study. Matthews was so accurate that the others said jokingly that he could carve faces on the shoulders of a lemonade bottle; Flanagan was peerless at lettering a tombstone. But they had their faults: Matthews was deplorable at foliage and Flanagan was hopeless at the angle-cut to get shadows. The foreman, Finucane, was the best all-round man in the province but he was unpredictable in mood, and if he were ill-tempered he couldn't carve soap. They were all superstitious to an extraordinary degree, and if a mallet fell from a scaffold every man on the job watched to see if its handle pointed to the gateway, for if it did there was trouble ahead. Their conversation was invariably trade-proud and esoteric; to a man they were contemptuous of tailors.

The boy again heard the footsteps behind him. Crunching on the limestone spalls. He knew immediately it was the foreman. The man stayed watching him for a moment before he spoke gruffly. His cap hid his eyes.

"Well, how're you doing?" The foreman was as lean as a mustang. He had a small brown moustache.

"Fine, sir."

"That's it! Go on, go on! What are you afraid of? You're working on the freeway." Finucane put his hand in behind one of the trestles and with his fingers caressed the foliage carved on one of the terminal bosses. This was his own work. On the boss were the letters I.H.S. on a bed of leaves. The caressing appeared to afford him keen satisfaction. Coming out in front of the doorway again he kicked the spalls away. "Keep the path clean underneath you and don't let people be dragging that stuff up the middle of the chapel," he said. Then he gave a grunt indicative of a grudged satisfaction of the boy's work.

As the foreman turned to go away he spoke with a half-smile. "Mother Xavier is in the garden — she's gathering more leaves." He turned down the short cement pathway that led to the road. As he walked away he kicked more of the spalls aside.

Finucane must have heard the nun coming, for scarcely had he gone than Mother Xavier came round the corner of the chapel with a great ado of hissing and trundling. She was a gigantic woman with an enormous, bespec-

tacled face. It was almost impossible to determine her
expression, as she had a trick of sealing up her eyes by
reflecting the sunlight on the lenses of her spectacles.
Her face was pale and the mouth indeterminate. The
tremendous girth of her body made playthings of her
rosary and girdle. Through the creakings of her approach
the boy made a last effort to sift the noises that he
fancied were coming from within the chapel. His effort
was unavailing, for no sound could be heard above the
clicking of the nun's rosary and the great rustle of her
moving garments. The boy looked down into the twin
circles of reflected sunlight that hid her eyes. Then he
saw that the old nun was carrying a handful of leaves.

"Aha, young man!" Mother Xavier wheezed. The boy
stopped working, and as a mark of respect dipped his
goggled forehead towards his mallet-head.

"Well, did you find out what kind of leaves they
were?"

"I did, ma'am—I think they're hop leaves."

"Hop leaves?" she complained. Grumbling, she moved
to one side and peered through the stilts of the trestles
at the foliage carved on the terminal boss. Then, "They
don't look like hop leaves to me. I don't know much
about hop leaves. Why didn't he put vine leaves or some
other kind of leaves on them?"

"I couldn't exactly say, ma'am."

"Tck-tck! Well, maybe he knows his own business.
And maybe he doesn't! Now isn't that a nice leaf?" She
was handing him up a sycamore leaf that was splendid
in its young green leaf and red stem. The boy took it
gravely and, catching it by the stem, revolved it apprais-
ingly between his thumb and forefinger.

"That's a lovely leaf, ma'am."

"And that?" She handed up another leaf.

"That's a grand leaf, too, ma'am."

"And that?—and that?—and that?"

The boy said they were all beautiful leaves.

"And will you tell me why he didn't put those leaves on the boss instead of his old hop leaves?"

The young stone-cutter said he couldn't exactly say.

Suddenly the great nun became conscious of the boy as a boy. Her face grew a shade softer.

"What's your name, sonny?" she asked.

"Jamesy Dunphy, ma'am."

"And where are you from?"

He told her that. Also his age. That his father and mother were alive. That he was the eldest of six. That his mother had had an operation for gall-stones. That the baby was as good as gold, except the time that he had the whooping-cough, when he got up any amount of phlegm. That he had an aunt a radiologist in an hospital in Lancaster. That his father had bound him to a stonemason. That he pulled the goggles down on his eyes when he was working on a certain class of stone.

This information received, the old nun delivered judgment. "God bless you, Jamesy, but you're a great boy altogether. Your father and mother should be proud of you!"

The boy had no reply to this, except to attempt a faint smile. This smile was killed decisively as he heard a low squeak from the chapel door. His sudden tautness communicated itself to the old nun, who immediately moved herself to a position where she could peer in the doorway. She continued to look in suspiciously. Just as she was about to investigate the squeak further two other nuns came walking out of the pathway that wandered through the flower-beds. One was a tall, graceful nun of thirty-five or so, who had the accurate features of statuary allied to the capital complexion of rude health. Her companion was a tiny old nun with a bright scarlet face so pointed that it instantly reminded one of a small song-bird. On catching sight of Mother Xavier this small old nun sprang to the attack. She turned her face to the tall nun beside her.

"There she is now, Reverend Mother, pestering the poor little boy," said tiny Mother Catherine.

Mother Xavier gathered herself for attack. Herself and Mother Catherine were old friends who played at being old foes. For many years they had taken every second term at being Reverend Mother. At last they had been successful in their pleadings for a younger nun in command. They were now testing the new Reverend Mother, playing at being enemies in her presence, simulating contrariness and even dotage; not infrequently taking refuge behind barriers of obtuseness in order to witness her reactions of perplexity. It was all a game, and the new Reverend Mother thoroughly understood the rules. She knew that the two old nuns were probing her for that kernel of royalty that must of necessity be present in every woman who seeks to rule a community of women.

So Mother Xavier, playing according to the rules of the game, bridled in the midst of her fat. She employed her old subterfuge of taking refuge behind the light-laden lenses of her spectacles. She tucked her leaves up her capacious sleeves, and mock-fumed at the venom of the little woman's onslaught.

"The Lord give me patience!" she breathed.

The young Reverend Mother extended her arms in a wholly delightful gesture. "Hush, mothers, hush!" she chided. The boy was tapping softly, one eye on the new-comers so as to be ready with his salute if they addressed him.

Then two traitorous leaves began to sneak down out of Mother Xavier's sleeves. They were buoyant and took a long time to fall to the ground. Mother Xavier saw their treachery reflected faithfully on Mother Catherine's face. Mother Catherine opened her mouth and made the preparatory noises of a song-bird who hears singing from afar. Her opponent pursed her mouth as a prelude to retaliation. The young Reverend Mother took them by

the arms and drew them softly away. "Something I wish
to ask you both . . ." she said. She guided them as a
dancer moves a partner. They seemed unwilling to part
company with their anger. As the three nuns moved
among the flower-beds the boy watched them curiously.
In his own mind he compared them to a hillock of black
serge on the move. He heard the two old voices clash on
one another; then the oil of the young nun's speech was
poured between.

When they had gone, the girls came out of the chapel.

One, a black-haired girl of fifteen or so, scurried skit-
tishly out from beneath the scaffold and rushed to the
doorway that led to the road. The other, a tall girl of
about seventeen, with ripe-corn hair bushing on her
shoulder blades, walked out slowly. She was obviously a
disdainful but graceful minx. Despite the apparent valour
of her carriage, the indefinable impression of unsureness
in calves and ankles was unmistakable.

Jamesy Dunphy lowered his hammer and eyed her
fully and severely. Watching her move away from him
he said nothing, for he was shrewd enough to know that
if he stayed motionless the girl would turn round. She
did so, a good deal sooner than he had expected. Finding
herself fully apprehended, she faced him as bold as brass.
The boy ran his hand down the moulding in the direction of the terminal boss, thereby subtly implying that
the carving of the foliage was his unaided work. The
tall girl was still staring. Their glances were locked for
a little while.

"D'you see me?" asked Jamesy. The words of themselves seemed harsh, but the intonation was soft.

"I do."

"You'll know me when you see me again."

More than a hint of her tongue appeared. "A cat can
look at a queen," she said.

"Can a cat fire stones at a queen?"

She looked around at the light spalls. "Stones!" she

said contemptuously.

A pause. The boy over-earnestly returned to his work. Again the sound of young footsteps behind him, picking their way among the spalls.

"What are you doing?" she asked.

"Can't you see what I'm doing?"

She was about four yards from him now. She was peering at the boss on the left-hand side of the door-way. "Did you do that?"

"Huh-huh!"

"You did in your eye!"

The boy said evenly, "And who do you think did it so?"

"You didn't do it — that's one sure thing!"

A pause. Then the boy spoke out of the corner of his mouth.

"Run away, little girl, and do your lessons!"

"Lessons? I'm in Intermediate!"

The boy's face creased in its film of powder. He said a curious thing. "Trace the character of Banquo."

Her eyebrows lifted in genuine amazement. "Did you do Inter.?"

"Uh-huh!"

"An' what are you doing picking old stones if you did Intermediate?"

The boy gave her a look of concentrated scorn.

"Here, buzz off!" he said.

"I'll buzz off if I like."

There was a sudden agitated whisper from the doorway at the roadway. "Kitty! Kitty Kavanagh! Reverend Mother is over in the playground. She's watching you."

A momentary wiggle of fear came into Kitty's eyes. She looked across the flower-beds and saw Reverend Mother walking up and down on the nearer edge of the school playground. She stepped backwards and placed the head of a bush in the line of vision between herself and the nun. "Ah, she can't see me at all." She threw the defiant words across her shoulder.

"She's after looking at you, Kitty," wailed the dark girl. Then in terror and uprighteousness, "I'm going away."

"Who's stopping you, cowardy-cat?"

But the young Reverend Mother had seen the girl. The speed of her gait increased as she debated within herself whether or not she should reprove Kitty Kavanagh for her forwardness. She found it difficult to reach a decision, for her own memory was harrying her without respite. Then, as now, it was a bright May morning. The slow, soft effervescence of the apple-blossom was foaming in the vat of the orchard; Bernard had come striding through the trees, his head every now and again was bending engagingly. She was picking rust off the garden seat with her finger-nail. Bernard came nearer and nearer, bringing with him the treasures of his carriage and eyes and hair. Again and again the vision sprang out from the ambush of the years. The young Reverend Mother groped for her beads and ran them through her fingers as she walked.

The Great Parlour was on the second storey of the convent. The lower half of the windows had been raised to their full extent so as to let in the May air. Within, the two old nuns were seated behind the table watching the young Reverend Mother and Kitty Kavanagh. Mechanical impulses of their lips compelled them to call the girl "Baggage! Minx! Madcap! Hussy!" but their imprecations had no validity. They continued to watch, with such immobility that they might have been sleepers. They were independent of eagerness and anger and surprise. Their souls were beyond invasion. Long ago they had made a truce with life, and life had respected the terms of the bargain. Now they were two old gentlewomen of God who were superior to the memories of tulle and music and huzzas. From their holy stupor they continued to watch as they had watched the village below them for more than fifty years. They knew themselves for what they were — two old leaks by which the tremendous confidences of tormented wives had been vented. They continued to watch, with such an extraordinary concentration as almost passed muster for obtuseness. But they were not obtuse. They had seen too many novices with smiling distances in their eyes, and finger-tips for ever seeking their ear-lobes. They had seen too many ringleted cherubs grow up and meet seduction, too many angular imps enlarge and become country empresses. They had strong precedents to guide them: they themselves had distilled lamplight on far hills and the litmus bloom of rhododendrons to inadequate drops in the eye-corners. They had recognized themselves in everyone with whom they came in contact, until personal pain was lessened by division and subdivision. A shot in the boundary elms would have startled them; a rat gnawing in the partition would have terrified them. But the remoter phenomena of people's emotions they perfectly understood.

Mother Xavier had now no sunlight to gild her glasses, and there behind the lenses was discovered the reason why she herself had been selected Reverend Mother. Now more than ever was Mother Catherine a bird of God. But what kind of bird was she? She was neither His falcon nor His magpie nor even His beloved black hen. Age had granted her the boon of interpreting aright the authenticity of curious hallelujahs. A slow, sad smile slitted her beak. She continued to regard Kitty Kavanagh, and, as she watched, she saw the girl's dead mother and dead grandmother stand behind, directly behind, the flirting child. Just so they had coquetted and pirouetted and flirted. And had they been the worse for it all? No, a thousand times no. (The soft silver gongs of first love were ringing through the sunny convent and were strangely welcome.)

The two old nuns continued to watch in stubby pattern, their etiolated faces framed in the black passe-partout of their veils and their facial bones thrown into relief by the light reflected from the inverted fans of their gamps. Their amazing power of self-identification was now being exerted to the full.

Just then the foreman stole past the dark-haired sentry at the gateway and took in the situation at a glance. He saw the boy and girl, the nuns behind the open window and the striding Reverend Mother. His decision was swift. "Hey, come off it!" he roared at the boy.

The girl stood, a cool spectator, enjoying the young-ster's shame. The foreman did not intimidate *her*. Her sense of amusement heightened as the boy went round the corner of the chapel, to work on large rough stones lying beside the gooseberry bushes. As he went he had the wit to hum to himself, "And I'll not forget you, darling, in the land I'm going to . . . ."

A breeze came up out of the good green fields. It prinked and pranced like a flighty filly. Suddenly it stood stock-still, and instantly the bright May morning was motionless. The young Reverend Mother moved up through the tulip beds on her way to the main door. Her face had the lustre of prayer-book gilt. The old nuns remained regardant until such time as the approaching nun was out of sight beneath them. Then each awoke to find that her mind had been a box within a box within a box.

King of the Bees

It was morning when Xandy, the young red-haired travelling-man, came over the crest of the road and looked down into the furze-brilliant lap of land that lay between him and the alive sea. Set haphazardly amid the lacy walls of small fields, thatched cottages gleamed lime-white in the May sunshine. The road on which he stood ran on a mile-and-a-half long ridge of ground and was lost for a moment of vision amid the grey shops of the village. On the hedges beside and beneath the traveller fuchsia leaves were still dark — the upland heather, too, was as yet unlighted by the splendid year.

Ignoring a boreen that fell away towards the sea-cliffs Xandy thrust swiftly onward. After a while he reached a ruined cabin on the seaward side of the road. The soft rain of the night before and the newly-minted morning sunlight following on its track had evoked the vinegary smell of soot and mortar and rotten thatch and nettle-bed from the space between the walls of the broken cabin.

Looking up, Xandy spied a bee-swarm hanging from a scrap of rafter that projected over the place where once the wicker of the inner chimney-breast wall had been. Dangling there, the swarm resembled a swallow's nest. Xandy's freckled face tightened with puckishness. Bee country this would be, he thought, after a glance at the fields below him, for, look!—here lay fuschia and clover and heather. Here, from time immemorial, the bees would have worn traditional lanes in the air.

For a while Xandy continued to watch the swarm; its nadir was alive with outriders scrawling in the air. Then, as a movement in the spread of land below him caught his attention, Xandy glanced downwards and descried a little man move limpingly to the top of a fence. His hands screening his eyes against the sunlight, this man began to scan the surrounding fields. Beside the watcher lay a bicycle and a timber box.

Again, glancing to the right, where, half a mile away, a similar boreen writhed through fields to the sea, Xandy saw another watcher — a heavy man, and a postman, too, if one were to judge by the sunlight striking his peaked cap. This second man was mounted on a piebald cob— across the pommel was hung a limp mail-sack. This man's eyes, too, were hand-screened against the sunlight. Glancing again from one to the other of the two men, Xandy laughed outright. With a gay flick of his thumb he lifted his hat and leaped on to the dike beside the cabin. He cupped his hands about his laughing mouth.

'Bee-e-e-s!' he halloo-ed into the bowl of the country-side. 'Bee-e-e-s!'

On hearing the cry, both the figures in the lowlands grew agitated. The small man hobbled down from the fence, cast himself at his bicycle and began to pedal furiously uphill towards the main road. The postman, too, lashed the cob's rump with the end of the reins and urged it against the incline.

A laughing girl, wearing a fawn shawl and carrying a market-basket across her arm — she was twenty at most — was now standing on the road behind Xandy.

'What are you laughing at, travelling-man?' the girl asked. The pleasantness of her face was enhanced by morning sunlight.

Xandy looked down from his perch.

'Money from the sky!' he said cheerily. He indicated the swarming bees.

'Ah!' the girl breathed, her lips shining apart. 'Bees! Hung, too, they are from the rafter of my grandfather's cabin.' She shook out her left arm from the tassels of her shawl. Xandy's gaze fell on her fingers that were free of rings.

The cyclist had gained the main road in the east; the

horseman the road in the west. They were coming towards the cabin, both riding at a furious rate.

'This one is Tailor Mullally,' the girl laughed, indicating the cyclist. 'And this—the almighty jockey on the horse —is Peter the Post. Bee-men, both. They'd drive a knife to the hilt in your back for a swarm o' bees!'

The fat postman was first on the scene; his back was stiff, yet with the dint of desperate riding his belly quivered like shaken blancmange. With a loud cry of 'Whoa!' he flung himself from the cob's back; then, tightening the strap of the old post-bag about his wrist, he waddled towards the bush-blocked gap that led to the cabin.

Straightaway, the angry tailor came up, tossed himself from the saddle of his bicycle, and grasping his timber box, moved hoppity-hop so as to insert himself in the gap by the side of the fat postman.

For a moment the two men were locked in the thorns of the narrow opening.

'*My* bees, postman!' The tailor spoke in a high falsetto.

'Liar!' The postman's voice was full and deep.

'Witness what he called me, stranger!' the tailor sang out.

Xandy shifted his weight from one leg to the other.

Still eyeing Xandy, the tailor pointed up at the bees. 'Witness, also,' he cried out, 'that my bees are branded!'

Tolerantly the postman pushed his rival aside. 'Bees branded!' He laughed richly, like a bass singer. 'Red raddle on their rumps, maybe, like boughten cattle at a fair'.

The tailor's face tightened with triumph. 'Not raddle, friend, but sprinkled flour as they were leaving my hive. See!'

With a quickening interest, Xandy and the girl glanced up: true—the swarm as a whole seemed dusted with white powder.

The postman's face registered a minor defeat. Then he

snorted. 'Whitewash from the old wall,' he said. 'The bees are mine!'

'Mine!'

'Mine, I say!'

'Mine! Mine! Mine!'

The conflict had drawn Xandy and the girl together. She whispered: 'The bees are on my grandfather's cottage. You'll not forget that, travellin'-man!'

'Sssh!' Xandy enjoined. 'Yours they'll be!'

High voice and low voice were now at it fast and harsh. The postman tore the bush from the gap and waddled into the ridged potato-sown field at the gable of the ruined cottage; thence he tried to find a way to come at the blind side of the swarm. Breathing heavily, he began to hoist himself on to the low dry-wall. As he did so, the tailor, his anger snapping like a twig, flung the wooden box at his rival.

The flat of the box struck the postman on the side of his head, sent his official cap skew-ways and revealed the full extent of his baldness. The blow caused him to stagger sideways for a step or two. Recovering, he adjusted his cap, clenched his great fists, crouched until he appeared to be all muscle rather than blubber, and then lumbered into the potato-garden in pursuit of his assailant.

Hither and thither the pair dodged on the ridged ground. The shortness of one of the tailor's legs was proving rather to his advantage, for, by keeping his shorter leg on the ridge and his longer leg on the furrow, he managed famously. Once, as the postman was almost upon him. the tailor turned in such a small compass as caused his pursuer to fall forward on the ridge. Then, as he struggled to rise, the postman rolled on to the broad of his back in the furrow and was trapped like a sheep in a gully.

The tailor ceased his skipping. He picked up a clod of

earth and flung it at the roaring postman. As Xandy
gave a cry of reprimand, the tailor snatched up his box
and leaped on to the dry-wall. Thence he started to
claw upwards on to the stout clay gable. Reaching a
point of vantage he lay full length on the wall and,
pulling his tweed cap over his eyes, set about capturing
the honey-drugged swarm.

Xandy laboriously dragged the heavy postman to his
feet. 'I'll skin him alive!' the fat fellow was roaring.

Shaking himself free of Xandy's arms the postman
lumbered across the furrows. At the gable-end his
breathing grew noisy as he noted that the tailor's legs
dangled well out of his reach. He then cast about him
for some weapon: finding none to his liking he rushed to
the back of the cottage and there thrust in by the gapped
doorway. Xandy came leaping close on his heels.

The tailor was on the very point of boxing the swarm.
The postman dragged up a handful of grass to which a
lump of rabbit-sand and mortar was adhering. This
missile he flung at the cluster of bees. The struck swarm
disintegrated. The tailor dropped his box and, still
jockeying the wall, pressed his hands over his ears and
pushed his face downwards against the dried clay.
Xandy, his fingers locked behind his ears, threw himself
down until his face was close to the rubble.

On the ground beneath his face Xandy saw three or
four fallen bees that clambered purposefully over the
rubble, as if in pursuit of an insect grail. Three of these
bees then converged upon the fourth. This central bee
seemed to differ from its fellows: it was slender, long and
torpedo-tailed. Its wings seemed inadequate for flight
and there was a positive yellowness on the underpart of
its body. Xandy bit back his cry of triumph. Here, under
his hand, was the queen bee.

Swiftly thrusting his hand into the pocket of his
tattered jacket, he emptied his matchbox; the three-
quarter-opened box he placed upside down on top of the

queen and then, carefully closing the box, trapped her.

Xandy reconnoitred the sky. All he could see was the high violent moving of dots. He rose to a crouch, then moved quickly out through the front doorway of the cabin and joined the girl on the roadway. 'Let us be going!' he said, indicating the distant village.

'You're leaving that pair to slaughter one another?' she asked incredulously.

'There isn't a solid blow between the pair of them,' Xandy said. He placed his hand into his pocket and dented the matchbox so as to give the queen air.

Xandy and the smiling girl had begun walking along the roadway. Snippets of conversation fell between them. Glancing over his shoulder, Xandy noticed that the mounted postman made a grotesque figure as, with his canvas sack covering his head, he rode into the west. The tailor, box on head, muttering angrily to himself, then cycled past them as they walked eastwards.

The pair of rivals left the main road and took separate boreens that ran downward to the sea. The swarm was still scattered in the sky. Now and again a single bee fashioned a figure-of-eight over Xandy and the girl as they moved in the direction of the village.

As they reached the first public-house at the village edge, the girl readied her shopping basket.

With a smile, Xandy said: 'If I treated you to a glass of wine I'd have to go drouthy myself!' The girl laughed her thanks. Xandy added: 'I'll own a sovereign within the hour—that I'll promise you!'

They entered the pub. To the dour publican, Xandy sang out: 'A pint of draught, there!' He slammed a silver coin on the counter.

The girl sauntered slowly to the grocery end of the shop where she entered into conversation with the publican's wife. Thereafter her eyes kept wandering towards the travelling-man. The publican's wife became quickly aware of the girl's preoccupation.

The woodwork of the bar was stained and varnished coffin-bright and the walls were distempered green. Behind the bar pewter vessels with glass bottoms hung from brass cup-hooks driven into the painted mock tuns. Through the back window the sunshine struck down in a short shaft to the white-sanded floor.

Waiting for his drink, Xandy seated himself on a stool by the wall and, taking out his matchbox, examined it intently. So engrossed was he in his examination that the long bald head and dark face of the publican emerging into brightness caught him unawares.

Setting the drink on the counter, 'See a swarm o' bees west the road, young fellow?' the publican enquired.

'That I did, now that you mention it!'

'And a pair o' men on their track?'

'One a fat fellow on horseback, the other a spancelled fellow on a rusty bike?'

'You have 'em! Which of 'em has the swarm?'

'Neither the one nor the other! They're still chasin' what belongs to me.'

'You!'

'Wild knows wild, publican!' Xandy spat his contempt to the sand.

The publican was momentarily taken aback. His wife and the girl ceased their conversation.

The sound of heavy horse's hooves broke the silence. After a few moments the postman, sweat-spots bright on his forehead, lumbered into the bar. Ignoring Xandy, he called for a drink. To the publican, he said: 'I'll have the law on him! My bees are gone mad through the sky.'

The publican grunted and turned away. The postman took his seat in a sunny corner inside Xandy.

Presently the lock-and-miss of a rusty bike was heard; the tailor, hobbling in, glared at his rival and then called out for a drink. He took his seat on the stool at the near side of Xandy, who, with his glass set securely on the seat beside him, was idly piercing the lid of his matchbox with the point of a snapped-off match. As a weak wing emerged from the box, Xandy carefully poked it back again.

The postman cleared his throat loudly: the tailor hawked furiously in the deeps of *his* throat. The pair eyed one another directly. As on a signal they set their drinks aside. The publican took up a mallet which he used for tapping barrels of stout and balancing it on one of its points on the high counter said: 'If one o' ye as much as mentions the word *bees* he'll have me to reckon with!'

Xandy flicked his grey hat upwards and began brightly: 'Aristotle was the wisest man who ever lived. Three things were beyond his understanding: the movement of the tides, the mind of a woman, and the laws that bees make in the governing of a hive.'

The tailor and the postman looked at him with angry interest.

Xandy took a sip from his glass and then went on: 'To me these things are an open book. Tides hang on the moon's pull, a woman is flawed by nature to yield to flattery. And . . .' He broke off abruptly.

'The bees?' the publican's wife prompted.

'That's a question delivered to the proper quarter. I was given power over bees. If I call bees, they answer.'

'Answer?' laughed the publican.

Xandy was tolerant. 'First they blacken the sky. When I call them closer, they descend like a tame hawk when he sees swung red meat.' Then, as a careless aside: 'Maybe I was here before!'

The tailor asked: 'Where, under God, were you before?'

'In this world.'

The publican broke the tension with a short nervous whinny.

The tailor said eagerly: 'Call down *my* bees, travellin'-man and I'll give you a half-sovereign.'

'*My* bees were always free of the Isle-of-Wight disease,' the postman bragged. 'Summon them down to *me,* stranger, and *I'll* give you a half-sovereign.'

'What'll *you* give to see a miracle?' Xandy smilingly enquired of the publican.

'A full sovereign,' the wife answered.

There was a moment's silence. 'Will you break your wife's word?' Xandy taunted.

'I'll not break her word,' the publican said; 'it's her back I'll break one of these night-oes!'

His wife's manner in no way indicated fear. The publican took the wagers from the tailor and the postman, then grunted as he added his own. By this time other villagers, young and old, had crowded in the open door.

Xandy finished his drink. 'Where'll I order the bees to swarm?' he asked the publican.

The publican looked around. With his index finger he drew a cross on the wet circle the travelling-man's glass had made as it was set down on the overhanging ledge of the bright counter. 'Summon the bees to swarm there!' he said.

Xandy took off his hat and with a sharp movement flung it on the seat behind him. Everyone present looked at his clean red hair and his good profile.

He walked to the counter. 'Back!' he shouted. All backed away. Then: 'I'll mark the spot with something that has my own smell on it,' he said, taking the matchbox from his pocket and placing it on the wet cross that diametered the wet ring. 'Open the window!' he ordered. Grumpily the publican obeyed.

Xandy walked to where the sunlight illuminated his face. Cupping his hands about his mouth, he shouted: 'Bee-e-e-e-s!'

Villagers continued to enter: they resembled actors entering on cue to take part in the climax of a drama. In the silence that followed an old man shut his hanging lips and said loudly: 'Once every century he comes! King Maoilre of the Bees is born again!'

The delay was long. A murmur of incredulity arose among the watchers. This Xandy lopped off by crying out: 'Silence! An outrider is coming!'

All eyes were firmly fixed on the sunny window. Suddenly the outrider was seen passing through: fluently it moved in the upper ale-brown air.

'By God!' swore the oldster.

First the bee essed aimlessly: then with a quick shadow-boxing movement as it fully experienced the powerful pull of what the box contained, it came down like a shot. The insect dropped to the counter and there crept forward towards the matchbox.

'One swallow doesn't make a summer!' the publican muttered.

'You clown!' Xandy said savagely. Then: 'Look!'

One—two—three—four bees were in the window! The crowd of gaping watchers drew backwards by a single silent step.

Then it was five—six—ten—twenty bees. Suddenly the loyal satellites came clouding and crowding in numbers beyond the power of counting. The open window was darkened with the scrawl of bees. They came like fistfuls of berries flung; like bubbles rising on a boil of broth. Purposefully and angrily they hastened, their instinct powerful as a religion.

Fierce in the attributes of peace the bees came mauling forward, each small winged item taut with the inherited lunacy of bee-history. Duty-fond and all-ignoring they were: they were God-postulating and well-winged. They were crammed tight with passion.

The booty-turgid weight of the swarm spilled over to form a brown beard; this grew perilously pendent, then base-heavy. Finally it gave indication of a crazy elasticity, and despite the fact that turn and turn about it integrated and disintegrated it continued to convey to the watchers a sense of terrifying communal power.

His eyes firm upon the bees, Xandy spoke: 'I can hold them no longer! Take them now that they're ripe!'

The tailor licked his lips nervously: 'Take 'em, you!' he said in an undertone to his rival.

The postman rose and, keeping his eye fast on the swarm, moved away through the knot of watchers.

Making a strange noise in his nose, the tailor said: 'I'll not touch them either!' He, too, thrust out. Silent as ghosts the crowd followed the rivals on to the roadway outside.

Xandy laughed himself and the others out of trance. He looked up at the pretty shawled girl: 'I saw a bee-skip hanging from a doorway up the village,' he said. 'Will you take a present from me, girl bawn?'

The girl nodded.

Xandy then scooped the bees into the market-basket which the publican's wife had lined with brown paper. He thrust his hand amid the swarm and, secretly opening the matchbox, allowed the queen to crawl out and be enveloped in her subjects. He then tied brown paper about the rim of the basket.

'Here!' Xandy said, advancing with his gift. 'Bees are blessed—they covered the Sacred Host with wax in the Penal Days. They'll set a small start to your dowry. Tell 'em of the man who first stirs your soul with love. Put one on your husband's scythe-blade as he sets out for the fields—then your cattle will never lack mouthfuls of rich grass.'

Smiling oddly, the publican's wife beckoned the pair into her green hallway. Grasping the girl's forearm, the woman also laid her hand along the travelling-man's arm. Her twitching lips were gone from discipline. 'The pair o' ye,' she said, holding them at arm's length. 'It would be small labour to set a roof on the broken cabin. Well, now?'

Xandy looked at the girl. His eyes fell. 'The curse o'

the road is on me,' he said in an unsure voice. Then, in his playboy tones: 'A swarm should not be trafficked for nothing! Come now, girl, pay me toll—a pin or a penny—else you'll break the luck that has been born between us.'

The girl's eyes were downcast. Then: 'I'll pay you,' she said softly, 'in the best o' coin.' Handing the publican's wife her basket, she kissed the travelling-man fully.

As the shawl fell limply on the ground, Xandy's arms tightened around the girl. They hung together as though they lived in dream. The publican's wife was filled with happiness. At last the girl broke away.

Xandy said harshly: 'I'll be off now—there's adventure like this at every turn of the road.'

'Not like this!'—the publican's wife was speaking in blotched, angry tones.

'Well, not like this!' Xandy conceded. He turned, and, walking firmly through the bar, went out through the shop door.

'Your wager!' the publican called out.

Xandy shrugged but did not reply.

Standing at the hall doorway the women watched him go. He passed under the bee-skip, then shrugged himself free of houses and faced for the bluff beyond which outer Ireland lay prone.

The Ring

I should like you to have known my grandmother. She was my mother's mother, and as I remember her she was a widow with a warm farm in the Kickham country in Tipperary. Her land was on the southern slope of a hill, and there it drank in the sun which, to me, seemed always to be balanced on the teeth of the Galtees. Each year I spent the greater part of my summer holidays at my grandmother's place. It was a great change for me to leave our home in a bitter sea-coast village in Kerry and visit my grandmother's. Why, man, the grass gone to waste on a hundred yards of the roadside in Tipperary was as much as you'd find in a dozen of our sea-poisoned fields. I always thought it a pity to see all that fine grass go to waste by the verge of the road. I think so still.

Although my Uncle Con was married, my grandmother held the whip hand in the farm. At the particular time I am trying to recall, the first child was in the cradle. (Ah, how time has galloped away! That child is now a nun in a Convent on the Seychelles Islands.) My Uncle Con's wife, my Aunt Annie, was a gentle, delicate girl who was only charmed in herself to have somebody to assume the responsibility of the place. Which was just as well indeed, considering the nature of woman my grandmother was. Since that time when her husband's horse had walked into the farmyard unguided, with my grandfather, Martin Dermody, dead in the body of the car, her heart had turned to stone in her breast. Small wonder to that turning, since she was left with six young children — five girls and one boy, my Uncle Con. But she faced the world bravely and did well by them all. Ah! but she was hard, main hard.

Once at a race-meeting I picked up a jockey's crop. When I balanced it on my palm it reminded me of my grandmother. Once I had a twenty-two pound salmon laced to sixteen feet of Castleconnell greenheart; the rod reminded me of my grandmother. True, like crop and rod, she had an element of flexibility, but like them there was no trace of fragility. Now after all these years I cannot recall her person clearly; to me she is but something tall and dark and austere. But lately I see her character with a greater clarity. Now I understand things that puzzled me when I was a boy. Towards me she displayed a certain black affection. Oh, but I made her laugh warmly once. That was when I told her of the man who had stopped me on the road beyond the limekiln and asked me if I were a grandson of Martin Dermody. Inflating with a shy pride, I had told him that I was. He then gave me a shilling and said: "Maybe you're called Martin after your grandfather?" "No," I said, "I'm called Con after my Uncle Con." It was then my grandmother had laughed a little warmly. But my Uncle Con caught me under the armpits, tousled my hair and said I was a clever Kerry rascal.

The solitary occasion on which I remember her to have shown emotion was remarkable. Maybe remarkable isn't the proper word; obscene would be closer to the mark. Obscene I would have thought of it then, had I known the meaning of the word. To-day I think it merely pathetic.

How was it that it all started? Yes, there was I with my bare legs trailing from the heel of a loaded hay-float. I was watching the broad silver parallels we were leaving in the clean after-grass. My Uncle Con was standing in the front of the float guiding the mare. Drawing in the hay to the hayshed we were. Already we had a pillar and a half of the hayshed filled. My grandmother was up on the hay, forking the lighter trusses. The servant-boy was handling the heavier forkfuls. A neighbour was throwing it up to them.

When the float stopped at the hayshed I noticed that

something was amiss. For one thing the man on the hay was idle, as indeed was the man on the ground. My grandmother was on the ground, looking at the hay with cold calculating eyes. She turned to my Uncle Con.

"Draw in no more hay, Con," she said. "I've lost my wedding ring."

"Where? In the hay?" he queried.

"Yes, in the hay."

"But I thought you had a keeper?"

"I've lost the keeper, too. My hands are getting thin."

"The story could be worse," he commented.

My grandmother did not reply for a little while. She was eyeing the stack with enmity.

" 'Tis in that half-pillar," she said at last. "I must look for it."

"You've a job before you, mother," said Uncle Con.

She spoke to the servant-boy and the neighbour. "Go down and shake out those couple of pikes at the end of the Bog Meadow," she ordered. "They're heating in the centre."

"Can't we be drawing in to the idle pillar, mother?" my Uncle Con asked gently.

"No, Con," she answered. "I'll be putting the hay from the middle pillar there."

The drawing-in was over for the day. That was about four o'clock in the afternoon. Before she tackled the half-pillar my grandmother went down on her hands and knees and started to search the loose hay in the idle pillar. She searched wisp by wisp, even sop by sop. My Uncle Con beckoned to me to come away. Anyway, we knew she'd stop at six o'clock. "Six to six" was her motto for working hours. She never broke that rule.

That was a Monday evening. On Tuesday we offered to help — my Uncle Con and I. She was down on her knees when we asked her. "No, no," she said abruptly. Then, by way of explanation, when she saw that we were crestfallen: "You see, if we didn't find it I'd be worried that ye didn't search as carefully as ye should, and I'd have no peace of mind until I had searched it all over again." So she worked hard all day, breaking off only for her meals and stopping sharp at six o'clock.

By Wednesday evening she had made a fair gap in the hay but had found no ring. Now and again during the day we used to go down to see if she had had any success. She was very wan in the face when she stopped in the evening.

On Thursday morning her face was still more strained and drawn. She seemed reluctant to leave the rick even to take her meals. What little she ate seemed like so much dust in her mouth. We took down tea to her several times during the day.

By Friday the house was on edge. My Uncle Con spoke guardedly to her at dinner-time. "This will set us back a graydle, mother," he said. "I know, son; I know, son; I know," was all she said in reply.

Saturday came and the strain was unendurable. About three o'clock in the afternoon she found the keeper. We had been watching her in turns from the kitchen window. I remember my uncle's face lighting up and his saying, "Glory, she's found it!" But he drew a long breath when again she started burrowing feverishly in the hay. Then we knew it was only the keeper. We didn't run out at all. We waited till she came in at six o'clock. There were times between three and six when our three heads were together at the small window watching her. I was thinking she was like a mouse nibbling at a giant's loaf.

At six she came in and said, "I found the keeper." After her tea she couldn't stay still. She fidgeted around the kitchen for an hour or so. Then, "Laws were made to be broken," said my grandmother with a brittle bravery, and she stalked out to the hayshed. Again we watched her.

Coming on for dusk she returned and lighted a stable lantern and went back to resume her search. Nobody crossed her. We didn't say yes, aye or no to her. After a time my Uncle Con took her heavy coat off the rack and went down and threw it across her shoulders. I was with him. "There's a touch of frost there to-night, mother," said my Uncle Con.

We loitered for a while in the darkness outside the ring of her lantern's light. But she resented our pitying eyes, so we went in. We sat around the big fire waiting — Uncle Con, Aunt Annie and I. That was the lonely waiting — without speaking — just as if we were waiting for an old person to die or for a child to come into the world. Near twelve we heard her step on the cobbles. 'Twas typical of my grandmother that she placed the lantern on the ledge of the dresser and quenched the candle in it before she spoke to us.

"I found it," she said. The words dropped out of her drawn face.

"Get hot milk for my mother, Annie," said Uncle Con briskly.

My grandmother sat by the fire, a little to one side. Her face was as cold as death. I kept watching her like a hawk but her eyes didn't even flicker. The wedding ring was inside its keeper, and my grandmother kept twirling it round and round with the fingers of her right hand.

Suddenly, as if ashamed of her fingers' betrayal, she hid her hands under her check apron. Then, unpredictably, the fists under the apron came up to meet her face, and her face bent down to meet the fists in the apron. "Oh, Martin, Martin," she sobbed, and then she cried like the rain.

The Bull Buyers

June came with a flash of flame. Heat rose in waves from the barley fields. Cows stood in streams to cool themselves. Bulls bellowed with a sense of maleness and menace.

Day after day, Peter the Bull Buyer, his twin brother Paul leaning over his shoulder, scanned the newspapers. But as June day followed June day their unwonted expenditure on newspapers seemed fruitless. At last, to their unholy delight, the pair read in an obscure corner of the paper that a farmer living in the extreme southwest of the county had been savaged by his own bull and had been removed in a serious condition to the local cottage hospital.

Three days later, feverishly running his stubby forefinger down the death columns of the same newspaper Peter read that the farmer, "his passing deeply mourned by his sorrowing wife," had succumbed to his injuries. On the day of the interment the pair set off in their shabby green van: they stopped some distance from the home of the deceased to make discreet enquiries. Then about three hours after the burial the brothers drew up beside a long low thatched farmhouse lying in snug pastureland on the southern slope of a hill.

Leaving his brother Paul waiting in the cab, Peter strode into the kitchen. There he took off his hat, beat it against his knee in mock anguish, and addressing a woman obviously the widow, who was seated demurely in a chair, asked loudly, "Is Jim buried?"

Two neighbouring women, the only others present and both on the point of departure, turned for a moment to listen.

"He is!" the widow said.

Peter drew out a red clotted handkerchief, turned his

head away and wiped his eyes. "I came as quick as I could," he said with a sob.

"Who would you be, decent man?" the widow asked.

Peter turned in mock indignation. "Jim's mother was a Neeligan. Right?"

"Right!"

"My grandmother was a Neeligan! Blood, ma'am, is thicker than water." Again he dabbed the handkerchief to his eyes.

"We must be off," said the pair of neighbouring women with one voice.

"I'll make a drop of tea for you," the widow said to Peter when the women had gone.

"A drop of tea, is it?"

"A drop of whiskey, if it's more to your liking."

"Whiskey I'll drink in honour of him that's gone," Peter said stoutly.

"Is there someone with you?" the widow asked with a glance through the window at the green van. "My brother, Paul," Peter said. "But he's all right where he is. He's not . . . crafty—if you understand."

The glass of whiskey in his hand, Peter sat down on a chair on the opposite side of the hearth from the widow. He slammed his hat on his right knee and looked morosely into the empty fireplace. "Lord have mercy on the dead," he said loudly, then drawing himself upright, he swallowed half the drink with a strong gulp.

Then he leaned forward and said in a conspiratorial whisper:

"Bulls are dangerous boyos!"

"Not if you handle them properly," the widow said primly.

"You never know the minute they'll turn and flatten you against a wall. Bsssh! You're a goner!"

"Proper precautions!" said the widow.

"You can never tell what goes on inside a bull's skull. He thinks, ma'am, if you'll pardon the expression, that someone is going to come between him and the cow!"

"The bull that killed my Jim, I found him as quiet as a child."

"You did!"

"I could catch him by the nose-ring and lead him around the yard the same as if he was a fat old cocker dog."

"And he never turned on you?"

"Never in his whole life."

"Say what you like, they're treacherous lads."

"I didn't find this bull so."

"You didn't?"

"If he was in a tantrum below there at the fence and if he saw me at the back door with the sweeping brush in my hand he'd leave this terrified yowl out of him and race bellowing up the field. Maybe he'd come back an hour or two later with a look on his face as if he was begging my pardon. I'd go and rub his wet nose and then the pair of us'd be friends again."

"You couldn't do that now after he's made a lone woman out of you?"

"I could indeed. If I had any grievance against the animal wouldn't I be making him out to be Christian like me and you. The next thing is I'd be asking him to keep the Ten Commandments!"

The widow smiled in a way that came close to being a laugh.

Peter was a little put-out by this practical approach. As again he raised the glass to his lips he eyed the widow more narrowly than before.

There was a beep on the car-horn. "The brother is anxious to be off," Peter said. "Could I have a look at the bull before I go?"

"Of course!"

The pair went out the back door, moved under a cluster of apple trees and reached a timber gateway that led to a neat enclosed paddock. The Hereford bull, standing alone and morose at the farthest corner of the field began to lumber towards the pair standing at the gate.

"A ferocious-looking beast," the bull-buyer said.

"Daisy! Daisy!" the widow said, rustling her fingers and calling the bull.

"I'd get rid of him if I were you! He might only attack a neighbour's child!"

"There are no children around here. Daisy! Daisy!"

The bull came slowly forward. He came to a stop five or six yards away from the gate and glared at the two. "He won't come to me while you're here," the widow said. "Daisy! Daisy! Daisy!"

"I'll tell you what I'll do," Peter said. "Even though I have a poor chance of selling him again I'll give you £50 for the bull and take the weight off your mind."

"That's only a quarter of what he's worth," the widow said quietly.

"It's not the full value — I admit. But who'd buy him from you except a fool like me?"

"I was sitting in the deadhouse of the hospital, right beside the head of the corpse of my dear husband, and I had a better offer than that!" the widow said.

"You had?"

"The long sod wasn't rolled on the grave before another man called me aside and doubled it. And a certain butcher will be here before dark to make me a better offer still."

"Are you in earnest, woman?"

"I'm in dead earnest. Butchers go wild for a bull that has done the likes of that."

"They do?"

"When they're choppin' up the meat they whisper into the woman-customer's ear what the bull did — by the way as a secret. The shop is thronged within the hour— spinsters mostly."

"You're jokin', woman!"

"If I'm jokin', you must know nothing about life. Did

you ever hear of people offering big money for the rope with which a man has hanged himself? To use it as a cure for a toothache!"

"Never!"

"There you are! Daisy! Daisy! Daisy!"

There was a peremptory beep from the car-horn. Peter muttered to himself, then said aloud, "Here, I'll give you the even £100 and have done with it!" He took a roll of notes out of his pocket.

"You'll do nothing of the kind, my good man. You might only beggar yourself, your wife and your children."

"I have no wife and no children."

"Haven't you now?" the widow said thoughtfully, at the same time looking Peter up and down. Then turning away: "Daisy! Daisy! Daisy!"

"Are we goin' to do business, me and you?"

"What class of business are you talking about?"

"Buying and selling the bull, of course."

"Oh, that class of business! Money isn't everything," she said meaningfully. Then: "Daisy! Daisy!"

Peter stood back. He looked from the bull to the woman. He suddenly saw that the widow was younger than he had imagined. He also seemed to be weighing both in his mind. He beat on the stony clay around the gate with the knobby end of his ash stick. He glared back towards the house from whence the car horn was beeping furiously. It was the first deal of his life that had thrown him off balance. All his days had been spent matching his wits against cunning smallholders and now he found himself unable to cope with a widow who could gaze so tolerantly on the animal that had ended her married life. Sweating profusely, he looked at the bull's powerful head and horns, its eyes that had a barely concealed savagery evident beneath their glaze, at the wet nose with the ring dripping with saliva, and tried hard not to imagine the great bulk of the beast hurled at his own body. Even as he winced, he looked down at the composed face of the widow and was exceedingly puzzled. He was not revolted, of that he was sure: it was just that he felt aggrieved with himself at having failed to foresee just this reaction on the woman's part, and thus found himself unprepared to parry it. The farthest he could could go towards comprehension was that here was a woman who, in addition to possessing a shrewd mind, possessed rare and unpredictable avenues of feeling. She was like good earth that seemed to be calling out to be tilled. Thoughtfully, Peter stumped by her side back to the kitchen; there he stood facing her, his face a good deal softer than it had appeared on his entry to the kitchen. As again the horn beeped, he cursed with picturesque obscenity. The widow smiled tolerantly at his outburst.

"I'll tell you what," the bull-buyer blurted at last. "I'll drive my brother home and come back here by myself in a week or so and make a deal with you."

"Don't leave it too late!" the widow said archly, "or I might have a bargain struck with some other man."

"Don't clinch the deal without hearing my final offer! I can't talk my mind with that fellow pounding on the horn."

"You know the situation!" the widow said. "It's up to yourself!"

"I know! I know! Let us say that me and you have an understanding . . ."

"About what?"

"About the bull."

"The bull, is it?"

"About other matters too. We'll leave it at that, decent woman, and we won't either add to it nor substract from it. I'll come back the day after tomorrow alone and by myself, and we'll thresh the whole matter out. Maybe tomorrow would be better?"

"As you mention it, it might be better if you came tomorrow!" the widow said as Peter went out the door.

"What the hell kept you?" Paul wanted to know. "You'd have bought forty bulls in that time!"

As they rode towards the main road Peter was thoughtful. Now and again he raised himself from his seat to look over the hedges. Arrived at the road he looked back at the farm house nestling in its grove of trees.

"The poor woman was prostrate with grief!" he told his brother.

"Prostrate with what?"

"With grief! I could make no hand of her at all. And your beep-eeping on the bloody horn didn't help matters."

For some time the pair rode along in silence. Suddenly Peter looked sidelong at his brother Paul. Speaking softly, he said, "Supposin' I was to pull out of the home place, and leave you in sole possession, how much money would you consider that worth?"

"Oho!" said the brother. "So that's how prostrate the widow was!"

"How much?"

"Twenty-five hundred pounds."

"I'll see you in hell first!"

All the way home the brothers shouted and argued. They yelled sporadically at one another all evening: the row flared up during supper: at last at midnight in mid-kitchen the bargain was struck and clenched in traditional fashion by striking spit-wet palm on spit-wet palm. As an afterthought Peter was to have the green van: Paul was to buy another: there were minor financial adjustments as a consequence of this decision.

Fully satisfied, the pair went to bed. They slept in single iron beds in the one room in the cottage. Towards morning, Paul awoke and raised himself on his elbow. His brother was talking in his sleep — something he had never done before. Glancing across he saw that his brother's hand was extended fully from under the bedclothes and that the fingers were rustling. Straining forward to hear, Paul heard his brother's lips repeating in a soft, almost womanish voice, "Daisy! Daisy! Daisy!"

The Kings Asleep in the Ground

One day during a break in the half-hour allowed us for exercise round the top tier of A wing, Packy McSwiney of Bloody Foreland called for attention. Standing in front of the bearded naked men, he began to read in Gaelic from a scrap of blue notepaper.

I was squatting by the wall. The weak sunlight filtering through the long window in the roof was touching my tilted face. I did not bother to look up at Packy for I was tired, sick and cold.

For fifty-one days now we sentenced men had been on nudist strike for political treatment: it looked as if the strike would go on for ever.

I was tired, sick and cold. Tired of the prison sweats in the yard below who, in the subtlest ways, lost no opportunity of ragging us political prisoners. Sick to death of the clotted swab on my throat where Callaghan of Portumna had lanced a gland with a penknife. Sick to the heart of never being able to see a young woman sway away from me; sick to the soul of the thoughts poor food kept distilling in my head. Cold. Cold even in that mild April weather with the mark a Northern winter had set in my Southern blood.

Tired, sick and cold.

Packy, tall and gaunt, his eyes carrying the stare of the fanatic. A tuft of grey hair leaping northwest from the bare horseshoe of his upper brow to match the tuft between his goose-fleshed breasts.

'*A Cháirde*,' he began.

'Krrck!' someone said.

One or two of the men glared hard at McCarthy.

'*A Cháirde*,' Packy resumed, with a hint of menace in his voice, '*Dia Luain seo chughainn beidh . . .*'

He went on to say that on the following Monday we

145

Republican prisoners would have a debate in Gaelic on the clan system in ancient Ireland.

The hairy men nodded an indifferent assent. O'Brien, the warder, smiled and strolled away.

Finished reading, Packy crouched before me. 'You all right, Patcheen, boy?' he whispered.

Staring into the cleft where his navel had its hide, I nodded.

'Ye had a great clan, son. The O'Connors of Kerry fought against the Danes at Clontarf in the year 1014.'

Again I nodded. Within myself, I wailed: 'Oh, my God!' Then swiftly in my head, like the series of pictures that comes racing out of one of those little books a boy thumbs at the corners, I went over it all again . . .

The bus; my toecapping the parcel of printed 'memos' past an empty seat until I drove it among the old woman's parcels. Then seven, eight, nine miles of easy riding. The stab of concern as a secondary schoolboy boarded the bus a mile or two this side of the border and sat on the empty seat in front of me. My qualm vanishing as I recalled that, lacking a fuse, gelignite is only so much brown sugar. My feeling of relief replaced by one of bitterness as I realised that, at most, I was only a year or two older than the lad in the mono-grammed blazer.

Above the memory, Packy's voice droned on: 'Ye built Kyrie Eleison Abbey in O'Dorney, and Lislaughtin Abbey on the Shannon. Never forget that, Patcheen!'

The routine check at the border—the border Kerry-boy-me was going to smash so that Ireland would be united. The old woman grumbling as her parcels were turned over. I continued my staring at the loyalist weekly. Gradually the strain eased.

Then at the last minute with the bus on the move a big man had come leaping on to the footboard. Moving in, he took up a position facing the passengers. He was so tall that he had to stoop somewhat. His eyes fast on the old woman, he drew the glass slide and gave the driver an order. After a hundred yards or so the bus pulled off its direct route.

'Only for the foreigner setting father against son,' Packy was saying, 'ye'd be the last to yield to the dark invader.'

Halted outside the barracks, the bus was surrounded by uniformed men. A District Inspector jumped on board. He was followed by two constables.

'These yours?' the D.I. said to the old woman. He touched the parcels with his cane.

'Aye!'

'Come along!'

The old woman was hustled into the dayroom.

The tall man began to check our identity cards. Not a good mimic, I had been given a Southern name and a Dublin address. Emerging through the open upper quarter of the dayroom window, I could hear the old woman's voice. It had a note of hysteria in it. Yes, she was a Nationalist—she believed that the partition of her country should be ended.

I stood up.

'Where are *you* going?' the big man asked.

'Into the dayroom!'

Inside, the police looked up as I said abruptly: 'I take responsibility!'

'Claret was cheaper than paraffin oil, in the time of O'Connor of Carrigafoyle', Packy was proudly rhyming.

Five long, bitter years. In at nineteen, I'd be out at twenty-four. Five years of gold! What madness was in me then? What spell or rule was I under? Would I sell those years for a million quid? Not on your bloody life! And yet I had traded them for a single court-room statement. Compared with me, Don Quixote was a tower of wisdom. For had I not said: 'As a member of the Irish Republican Army, I deny the right of this tribunal . . .'

Et cetera.

Packy put his mouth close to my ear. 'Drift with it, son!' he said. 'If you fight against it, you're done!'

Again I nodded. The navel opened as Packy rose and went away. Remembering that he had spent fifteen years behind walls I watched him go. He borrowed a pin from O'Brien, the warder, and pinned the notice to the white-washed wall. The men kept shuffling along. No one bothered to stand and read the blue paper.

The bell rang.

Then it was beard after beard, red buttocks, varicose veins (like ivy coils), the remnant of one potbelly (now an old ballroom balloon), hammer-toe, lank shank and stallion flank, blue-glazed operation seam, brown mole, shaved poll, tender sole, ancient ulcer, not omitting one eye-shade. The last not an article of attire within the meaning of the act. Packy had given a ruling on that point.

The Governor had a spiky moustache which gleamed grey in his thin but choleric face. He wore a suit of dark material with a nondescript tie and white shirt. He was a decent-enough old skin within his limits.

For a while he puzzled over the blue notice. He turned it over and glanced at the back of it. He looked up at O'Brien, whose fleshy face was sweating.

'What does this say?'

'They're going to have a debate in Gaelic, sir.'

'On what subject?'

'On the clan system in ancient Ireland.'

'Will it be all right?'

'I couldn't say, sir.'

A pause. 'Limerick, eh, O'Brien?'

'Limerick, sir!'

'You're fairly fluent at this . . . Erse?'

'Middlin', sir.'

'You should be able to follow what they're saying?'

'If they kept to the Southern dialect, I'd make a fair

fist of it. But the minute I start to take notes, they'll
skeet to the Northern lingo. That's like chewin' rubber,
sir!'

The Governor pondered for a moment. 'Do your best,
O'Brien. Make a report.'

'Very well, sir.'

That night the pipe in my cell was speaking like hell
as Packy kept calling me up. I didn't answer. I pretended
to be asleep.

On the day of the debate instead of walking round the
top tier we padded into the Rec. Hall. On the rostrum
was a table on which stood a red plastic beaker. There
were two chairs — one for Packy; he was formally pro-
posed and seconded as chairman — the other for O'Brien,
the warder. O'Brien sat a little to the rear of Packy's
chair and had his arms folded across his chest. The other
warders at the back of the hall were mostly Northerners.
They were inclined to smile at O'Brien.

When we had taken our seats, Packy stood up fiercely
stern, and hawked in his throat. All of a sudden he
rounded on O'Brien: *'Bain díot do chaipín!'* he roared.

O'Brien jumped, then uncrossed his arms. The men
laughed—the warder's right hand had been holding a
pencil and his left hand a reporter's notebook. O'Brien
took off his cap and placed it on the floor beside him.
'Tóg bog é!' he advised Packy good-humouredly.

O'Brien's 'Take it easy!' made my mind revolt. How
could a man take it easy when now on the riverbank at
home the kids would be baiting lines and drawing in pink
trout? When now the hazels would begin to show form,
now the primroses, now the stitchwort, now all the things
that I so desperately loved.

The meeting came to order. McCarthy from Cork—he
had a rich brown beard with a mad stab of red in it—
was on his feet at once. Packy pounded him down.
McCarthy crumpled up a grubby scrap of paper and sat
down growling.

A thin man called O'Driscoll rose and began to enumerate the castles and conquests of his clan. He quoted at length from a poem in English on a raid of Algerian pirates on Baltimore, a town on the Southern coast.

Packy nodded his grudged approval of the use of English for the purpose of quotation.

Maguire of Fermanagh—he had a graveyard cough that pocked mid-tier all night long—mentioned the quartering of guests and gallowglasses, the payment of horse-boys and dog-boys, and the spreading of green rushes on the dining-room floor of the Maguire castles.

The Professor quoted Latin. Packy didn't quite approve of his stressing the theme of disunity among the clans. *'Omnes erant Cesares,'* the Professor said sorrowfully. *'Nemo censum dabat.'* He then went on to mention Louis the Fat wrestling with feudal disorder.

O'Sullivan of Bere said that when Don Juan Del Aquila had basely made peace with the English at Kinsale, and so had stained the sword of His Catholic Majesty of Spain, the O'Sullivans had banged the Catholic garrisons out of Berehaven, seized the munitions and despatched the eldest son of the clan as a hostage to the King of Spain to indicate their loyalty. This action had caused the Spanish King to conceive an abiding affection for the O'Sullivan clan.

But: 'Oh, my God!' I kept muttering. The bluebells and the stitchwort and the clumps of primroses at the end of the inchland where now for a certainty the sun was beating down with early-year ferocity. Oh, my God! the sandhills with the sea open and open and open.

Packy put in his spoke. He said that although his clan were feudatories of the O'Donnells, they claimed descent from Swaine, King of Norway, the ravager of the raven banner. The McSwineys were hereditary pipers, he said; the men had noses like eagles' beaks and the girls were handsome with fine foreheads and teeth.

McNamara of Tulla made reference to his predecessor,

Fireball, who had fought fifty-seven duels and had not been scathed by a single ball.

O'Rourke of Mayo mentioned mortar made of bullocks' blood and powdered oystershells. He spoke of spiral staircases with the twist sinistral, thus designed to give swordsmen the advantage of the right-handed blow.

Again McCarthy tried to make a statement but Packy seemed resolved to keep him out. *'Suigh síos!'* he roared as McCarthy rose to his feet.

Fitzgerald, O'Reilly, O'Malley, O'Neill, all spoke. An intense man named Loftus raised a wan cheer by saying that although he was a descendant of Cromwellian adventurers, his mother was an O'Byrne of Wicklow.

The debate had now got into a certain rhythm. Long since O'Brien the warder had ceased to take notes. Now he seemed fully bored.

But, Oh my God! already Ballynanty Wood would be coming alive and the rabbits begin to go hoppity-hop. The valerian, too, would be in bloom on the Abbey walls. What was I doing here, naked in a foot-smelling shed, listening to gibberish about dead chieftains? Was it for this I had traded clean linen, cocoa with a head on it, kids playing at hopscotch, salmon in the final of playing, and, above all, the long laze of blue waves. Oh, my God! I muttered over and over again in my mind.

I woke out of a haze to find Packy McSwiney looking straight down at me. The rest had fallen silent. 'There's a lad here without a word out of him,' Packy said quietly, 'and the last High King of All Ireland was Roderick of his name! Well, Patcheen? What have you to say?'

As I shook my head violently, my eyes misted and my senses spun. Again I shook my head to clear my brain of darkness.

McCarthy must have been waiting for just such a distraction. So firmly did he rise that no one could gainsay him. He glanced at the piece of paper in his hand, then glared at the warder on the platform. O'Brien lost his flabby look at once.

'When we McCarthys,' the speaker began, '—we who fashioned the beauty that is Cormac's Chapel on the Rock of Cashel, under our chieftains Dermot O'Donnell Mór and Finghin—were pouring out our blood in an effort to dislodge the Normans from Munster, we were basely attacked by the calf-choking O'Briens. This was in 1169.'

O'Brien stiffened. 'What are you saying out of that ugly mouth?' he blurted in English.

There was a chorus of cries. Some of the men stood up and shook their fists at O'Brien.

'*Ná bac an Béarla!*'

'*Labhair Gaeilge!*'

'*Cuirtear amach é!*'

With the men's rising, the smell of foot-sweat grew stronger.

O'Brien was on his feet, too. 'I want to say . . .' he roared. But again the crowd of prisoners shouted him down.

Two of the warders moved forward into the hall. O'Brien snarled them away. They lounged against the wall.

'*Tá go maith!*' O'Brien said easily, then went on in Gaelic: 'I want to say that on no lesser an authority than that of Giraldus Cambrensis, Dermot McCarthy was the first Irish king to swear loyalty to King Henry II of England. This was in Waterford in 1171.'

'You sheevra!' McCarthy roared. 'When the Normans broke into our beloved Desmond, we Cartys beat them at Gallen Glen, and thereafter we played the devil in Desmond. We had three great castles—Ballycarbery, Castlelough and the Palace. What had the lickspittle O'Briens in their hungry Thomand?'

An old man with a grey beard came to his feet. 'My mother was an O'Brien of Thomond,' he said in a deep voice. 'She told me for a fact that the McCarthys were violators of churches, murderers of kinsmen and ravishers of consecrated virgins.'

This statement brought cheers and boos.

'There's your answer!' Warder O'Brien roared.

McCarthy pushed idle chairs aside. 'I'll take on a traitorous O'Brien any day of the week!'

The warder dragged at his tunic. A button flew and hit the wall. Packy thumped the table for order.

'If you're going to fight him, O'Brien,' he said, 'you'll have to strip! It'll be fair pegging while I'm chairman.'

O'Brien tore off his shoes, then dragged at his trousers-belt. One of the other warders hurried up.

'Don't be a fule, O'Brien!' he said.

'None of your affair!' O'Brien was stepping out of his pants and underpants.

'You'll get the knock for this!'

'Mind the damned door!' O'Brien tugged his shirt over his head.

Stripped, O'Brien was seen to be a powerful man, but a soft one. As he padded down the steps at the side of the platform his white body quivered. McCarthy with his mad beard and dark skin had already taken up a fighting attitude in the space between the front row of chairs and the stage. The other prisoners had resolved into two groups of partisans—one for Desmond, the other for Thomond. Dull and listless I sat aside.

O'Brien shuffled in what was the memory of a boxing adolescence. McCarthy came to meet him. For a moment or two there was soft tapping. Then the men came crashing together. McCarthy drove in with a rigid fist that raised a weal on O'Brien's stomach. But as he emerged from the close-in, O'Brien fisted him heavily into the mouth and drew blood. 'How'd you like that?' O'Brien said from between clenched teeth as he shuffled away. The blood came spilling over McCarthy's split lip.

Again the contestants drew closer to one another. The bystanders urged them to go in and kill. 'Desmond!' one crowd shouted, 'Thomond!' the other. There was a sense of madness in the hall.

I came slowly to my feet. I began to scream. My mouth
set off of its own accord and I had no control over what
it was saying. I screamed of bluebells and pink trout. I
screamed of Kyrie Eleison Abbey. I screamed of the
schoolboy with the monogram on his blazer. I screamed
of the knife lancing my throat. I screamed the formula of
non-recognition. I screamed the satin sheen of a woman's
skin. I screamed Ireland free and united from the centre
to the sea. In Gaelic and in English I kept screaming.

The fighting stopped. The men were all around me
panting and urging me to put an end to my noise. But
I wouldn't stop because I couldn't stop. My voice was
careering away and dragging me in its wake. When at
last Packy put his hands on my shoulders I stopped.
There was an intense silence. One of the warders behind
us came tearing through. 'The Governor!' he shouted.

Packy pushed me down, then beat O'Brien in a race
for the platform. There he slung O'Brien's clothes behind
the curtain. 'Too late!' he yelled to O'Brien. 'Sit down!'

We all sat down. O'Brien sat in the middle of the men.
I found McCarthy next to me. His head was lowered and
he was spitting blood over his split lip. The spittle kept
dangling from the stab of red on his beard. Now and
again he drew his foot across the floor. He looked at me.
'It's a thing of nothing, Patcheen!' he said with an affectionate smile.

On the platform, Packy was himself once more.
'Poetry, Professor!' he said, with a glance at the door.

The Professor rose and began to declaim 'The Dead
at Clonmacnoise':

> *'In a quiet watered land, a land of roses,*
> *Stands Saint Kieran's city fair;*
> *And the warriors of Erin in their famous generations*
> *Slumber there.'*

Halfway through the second verse we saw the
Governor's entrance into the hall mirrored in Packy's

face. O'Brien crouched lower — the men nearest him leaned their elbows on the back of his chair.

The Professor's voice poured on. In it I found a strange healing.

> *Many and many a son of Conn the Hundred-Fighter*
> *In the red earth lies at rest . . .'*

The Governor walked noiselessly by the wall. 'O'Brien?' I heard him whisper to one of the warders.

'The Irish lecture is over, sir.'

The Professor was now reciting "The Fort of Rathangan':

> *'The fort over against the oak-wood,*
> *Once it was Bruidge's, it was Cathal's,*
> *It was Aaedh's, it was Ailill's,*
> *It was Conaing's, it was Cuiline's,*
> *And it was Maelduin's;*
> *The fort remains after each in his turn*
> *And the Kings asleep in the ground.'*

I came slowly to the warmth and to the light and the beauty. Within myself, I kept repeating: 'And the Kings asleep in the ground.'

The little poem had ended. Advancing shyly, the Governor coughed for attention. Packy held up his hand. The Professor shrugged and sat down. The Governor took up a position a little to one side of us.

'Mr. Chairman and gentlemen,' he said.

His eyes ran over our lines; I thought that his gaze rested overlong on the white shoulders of O'Brien.

'I have an announcement to make. The fact is, you see, I have received a message, a communication, that you have been granted political treatment. You may put on your own clothes as soon as you will. Thank you, Mr. Chairman and gentlemen.'

The Governor coughed and went away.

Packy slumped into his chair. He began to look steadily into the hollow of his hand.

We remained there wholly without movement. At last O'Brien came to his feet. Slowly he padded up the steps, pulled out his clothes from beneath the curtain and began to drag them on. As he did so, he glanced first at Packy, then at us. Thoughtfully he laced his shoes. He was struggling with the clip of his collar when the bell rang. Still we made no move. The Northern warders hung back. They looked at O'Brien. Suddenly we were all looking at O'Brien who had now bulked big—bigger even than Packy.

O'Brien walked to the platform's edge. He ran his eyes over our faces. Of a sudden he snapped out in Gaelic:

'*Go réidh!*'

We readied ourselves. Stiffly.

'*Seasaigí!*'

We stood. Proudly.

'*Iompaigí!*'

We turned. Rebelliously.

'*Siúlaigí!*'

We walked. Defiantly.

I walked with the rest. Then again it was beard after beard, red buttocks, varicose veins, pot belly, hammer toe, lank shank and stallion flank, shaved poll and ancient ulcer, all present and correct down to the single eye-shade with to-day's addition of split lip, one.

As McCarthy passed stiffly by, O'Brien winked at him. McCarthy returned the salute with a grin from his battered mouth. Inside myself I was thronged with warmth and light and beauty. I had sloughed the treachery of April and had once again begun to be ruled by the Kings asleep in the ground.